THE COVER UP

OSCAR SPARROW

DEDICATION

To the unbelievers. You guard the freedom to believe.

CONTENTS

FOREWORD FROM OSCAR

I am an English author and regret I have not had the education in life to write the superior form of English spoken in the USA.

1 CHAPTER ONE

"My brother's company has seven – *yes seven* – fucking container loads of Frankie Ferret merchandise on a ship two days out of Liverpool," said the prime minister, his face white with rage as he slammed his fist onto the table. The other members of the COBRA Committee exchanged hasty edgy glances, no one wanting to speak. Their leader waved a dismissive hand at the room. "Stupid, stupid bastards the lot of you. We can get the plebs through Brexit but there's no way – just no fucking way – we can lead this race of heroes through the death of Frankie Ferret."

He ran his hand back through his dishevelled hair and let his head droop forward in despair. The silence was broken by a gentle sobbing.

"My little ones are broken," whispered Alexana Fudge, Minister for Transitions at the Ministry of Chromosomes. "There's been no sleep since the news broke."

A senior female civil servant from the Ministry of Spin reached out across the table and took his hand.

"We feel you. We hear you. We hold you," she said.

Alexana Fudge let out a wail of helpless anguish and ran

from the room.

The prime minister re-found his track and passion.

"Keep that fucking wet rag out of my sight. Commissioner – let's hear it from you – what, what, what is happening?"

Dame Iona Peniston, the head of the Metropolitan Police, was a deep-voiced woman of about fifty, who chose to stand to attention as she spoke.

"For the record we all know that Frankie Ferret is a pre-school TV show, starring a ferret called Frankie, based on a children's story by a lewd pornographic hack novelist called Emma Calin. The concept has been franchised into cartoons, comics, films and merchandise in nearly every country on earth. The value to the world economy is about four hundred and eighty billion pounds."

"Including China," boomed the foreign secretary. "That bloody despot Kung Po Ginseng was on the phone an hour ago. He's going to invade Hong Kong and seize Sackman-Platinum bank if we don't fix this mess. Half of their exports are Frankie shit and their plebs are either rioting or too distressed to report to their sweat shops."

"Someone tell me why we can't just use some other ferret?" asked the PM.

"Cos few ferrets can speak, and even fewer are vegans," replied the civil servant from the Ministry of Spin.

"Look you drongs, no fucking ferret can speak."

The official gave her leader a withering look and spoke in a teacherly tone.

"I know that, you know that but the mob out there – including the Queen – do not know that. We wanted a new British brand, jobs, hope and joy for the pill-popping obese hordes. When the Pope set up a mass for the wretched animal and some fifteen-year-old kid swore she heard him say 'Amen', they made her a saint. No one was complaining when we spun the story. Gretchen Thunderbird is now on a world-saving tour, crawling through underground tunnels to save carbon pollution. The Vatican sold seven hundred thousand ferret rosaries and talking Frankies in furry capuchin monk robes. Three virgins in Milan claim they became pregnant after wearing Frankie-branded panties. We spun that so big that the miracle committee is on the verge of signing it off as verified."

"And then some white-van-driving-numpty lets the bloody creature escape from its cage in the middle of a traffic jam in Croydon," groaned the PM. "So just why can't we use another ferret?"

A large man with a severe public-school accent raised his hand.

"Prime Minister – Dickon Maltravers – Head of Intelligence. We all wanted facial and iris recognition technologies. If we put up a fake, it'll be spotted in seconds and the government will fall. The Trots, anarchists and a bunch of religious groups are anticipating such a trick and are ready to rebel. There were several diet extremists already getting some Twitter traction with a claim that Frankie ate rabbits. It's always the cover up that sinks you, sir."

"What about CGI? There's loads of Frankie footage."

"We're looking at that. We need time. There was a move by a powerful trans lobby to take Frankie through a gender transition. That was how he was going to remain immortal. He was on his way to the TV studios for the first episode with the vegan transsexual story line."

The prime minister slammed his fist once more into the table.

"I've just got a feeling that moron who let him go was some kind of gammon reactionary, probably egged on by that Morgan Peers. Bring the bastards in for interrogation commissioner. That bloody animal is out there somewhere. Get on and find it or clear your offices."

Police Inspector Crispin Bissel glanced at the BBC rolling news channel on the giant screen mounted on his Scotland Yard office wall. Hysterical mothers and sobbing children were being led to mobile counselling units, hastily fabricated from disused Brexit campaign buses. Baton-charging police confronted rioting and looting around toy and book shops. Things were bad but trouble always meant opportunity. His first in Politics, Philosophy and Economics from Oxford had equipped him perfectly for the role of officer-class desk cop. As a balding head popped round his partition, he realised his pork pie, Mars bar and latte coffee were spread openly on his desk.

"Caught you again Bissel," said Superintendent Bert Brickstone, pointing at the food.

"What? No? No, that's not mine – one of the junior assistants left it."

"Did they now. Fucking lucky then I'm here to eat it lad. Can't be doing with waste."

The older man picked up the pie and read the label.

"Says here this is for sharing – that's the PC way of saying that only a disgusting cynically obese bastard would eat all this himself. Sure you wouldn't like a bite, to save me from myself?"

"It's revolting – vile and barbaric. Once you're a vegan you can't contemplate such horror."

"Me neither, I can't bear to look at it any longer. I bet you've got a pot of fair-trade mustard hidden somewhere?"

The superintendent devoured the pie with a series of grunts and moans of almost orgasmic pleasure.

Inspector Bissel watched with horror and an agony of hunger. As a ruthless vegan *capo* in his friend group, his working life gave him the chance to escape into sin. Normally he could leave the office and sit on The Embankment with a pie, pasty or savoury slice hidden in a bag. He always made sure to walk back in to the office enjoying a stick of celery and drinking from a bottle of certified organic mineral water. How he hated Bert Brickstone. He was a throwback old bruiser, seeing out his time at a desk in the media relations hub. He made no secret of the bottle of whisky in his desk. He'd been a detective on the Sweeney Flying Squad until a barrel load of shotgun pellets had wrecked his knee, a fact he introduced during most encounters.

"If those robbing hard-man villains hadn't made me an untouchable hero Bissel, I'd be pissed up in the boozer with some old lags and maybe a decent old brass for a bit of nookie during siesta time. As it is, I'm just going to finish up that Mars Bar and that coffee."

"Yes, sir, I wasn't sure how to go near it to be honest."

"You're a stupid cunt Bissel. Why don't you come up to my office and have a snifter?"

"Sir?"

"Bissel – come to my office. This ferret crap can make you and it's in our lap. I can't bear the sight of you but you're the kind of twat we need."

"It's validating to feel called upon to make a difference

and commit personally to a more inclusive society, sir."

Bert Brickstone shook his head, muttering some dark words under his breath. Inspector Bissel followed his limping boss to his office, setting his mobile phone to record mode.

"Close the door and pick up that glass my Machiavellian young neo-puritan. I'm going to talk to you like a man so have the respect to listen like one."

The boss pulled a bottle of scotch from his drawer and slopped out generous rations. Crispin Bissel's heart pounded. He was being drawn into debauchery and corruption. His only chance of remaining pure was to acquiesce merely as a means of gathering evidence. He stared at the half pint tumbler.

"Well, get a slug of it then. If I drink alone, you'll be reporting me as a loner alcoholic won't you, and I know you'd like to?"

The young man affected a trembling half smile. He'd always hoped to avoid terror on this level. Feeling the fluttering of his anal sphincter he took a swig, hoping for courage.

"Did you know there's four hundred out of work actors who earn a living dressed up in Frankie Ferret suits at different venues? Did you know that Frankie Ferret World in the New Forest has just paid a million pounds for a roller coaster called 'Frankie's Drainpipe of Doom' and that it's booked for ten years? With the benefit of your education what's the plan?"

Crispin Bissel felt a sense of warmth and relaxation as he took another drink. He knew the outline of the emergency. He also knew that the police could grasp the Frankie flag and commit every resource to finding him. And if the *Bungling Bobbies Blew It,* in tabloid alliteration, anyone who'd suggested it would be dead meat for the ferrets. He could float the idea and let untouchable hero Bert Brickstone take the heat.

"Sir, we need to put the police centre stage. We can offer to deploy our own trauma counsellors to schools and community grief centres."

"Yeah, we can do all that soft shit for the snowflakes and self-publicizing celebrity victims but most of those people hate us as fascist pigs anyway."

Crispin Bissel winced. This was almost treason-level incorrectness. He had to remember he was using this encounter to gather evidence. He was feeling drunk.

"OK, we could set up specialist squads to attend any sightings and if necessary, get police divers into drains. The chances of finding it are very small, but media love police dogs and frogmen."

"Bissel, you've read my mind. We need a dynamic, young educated type who knows all the correct angles. We need the sad PR face and all the weasel words of caring like empathy, understanding, reaching out a hand to suffering communities, going an extra mile, standing strong for a friend, stepping up to feel your pain, slapping your pathetic faces because you're a load of bawling tossers."

"That last concept should do it, sir," slurred the young man.

"Sober up and get an extra star on your shoulder. You're now Chief Inspector, the *ferret loving face of the filth*. In an hour's time we'll put you in front of the press. Cometh the hour cometh the fall guy."

"Sir, I'm not sure –,"

"No one ever is. Here's my advice. You need glamour and allure. Get a couple of brasses, one blonde one ethnic to lead the teams. Get a bit of background and family stuff about the girls. No old-sweats or farting rude boy thicko coppers. No old gronk lezzers. You'd be better off with a couple of dogs, maybe a horse too – make sure they're pretty and the press get their names. Get it done and hope for a miracle."

3 CHAPTER THREE

Police constable Selena Fontesse moved back from the rain-spattered window of her Croydon bed-sit. The Polish girl downstairs was boiling cabbage again. She slumped down on her bed and flicked through the pages of her current romantic reading 'The Billionaire Stallion's Love Demand'. What she'd give to meet any kind of billionaire. *Carlo di Rigatoni* was holding his lover's hand as they strolled the sun-bleached sands of some stupid fucking island he owned. She threw it aside with a sigh. How had her life come to this? A stupid empty book of someone else's fantasy, the stink of cabbage, a sex life formed around her Frankie Ferret vibrator. All the reviews had said that once you turned to ferret, no rabbit would ever satisfy.

Everything was hype and the same ol' same ol'. The apparent loss of Frankie down a drain no more than a mile away in North End, Croydon, in the rush hour traffic two days ago, left her unmoved. The news that the hippy businessman, Sir Brandon Pickell had offered a million-pound reward for his safe return was slightly *more* interesting.

It was 4pm and her night shift didn't start until 10pm. She clicked on the TV news. The pictures were of her own police station, riot police facing down hooded crowds, many holding ferrets. A senior officer emerged and spoke through a loud hailer.

"My friends – please remain calm. So far twenty-eight people have been arrested for attempted deception because they have knowingly produced false ferrets. All animals submitted will be assessed by facial and DNA technology. Please consider carefully before you proceed."

There was uneasy shuffling and pulling of ugly faces by the mob. Cameras zoomed in on cute animals, one of which appeared to be wiping boot polish from its albino cheeks with gorgeous tiny paws. Within a few minutes the crowd had melted away to a line of white vans draped with England flags. She was sure one of the faces in the mob had looked familiar. Hadn't she been at drama school with him? A grave mannered sneery-voiced BBC reporter signed off the report.

"That's the shape of our society. This is Batty McKay on the grief-torn streets of Croydon."

She clicked off the screen. Surely no one would try to make the citizens look like dimbos, crooks and losers? Since she'd become a cop everything and every thought led to suspicion. How the hell had she gotten into this? She'd been doing OK as a webcam girl, specializing in vegetarians. One guy would even pay three pounds a minute to watch her hold bags of Puy lentils on her clitoris and whisper the words 'Chick Pea' while she sat on the toilet. It made the world a happier place. When her mum had been mugged and left with brain damage, she felt she had to step up. She formed a new bond with her mother who had forgotten she hated her. She filled in the forms, jumped the hoops and presented herself at the Hendon police training school. It was there she'd met Crispin Bissel, twelve years her junior, fresh out of Oxford University and on the accelerated promotion escalator. Poor tormented Crispin, a man longing for intercourse but afraid of envelopment by the female. During a liberal studies circular discussion led by Sergeant Karma they'd been encouraged to recover memories and cry on the person in the next seat. Crispin had admitted he was sexually aroused by falafels and let his tears fall on her. He left police school a very different man and was swept away to Scotland Yard. She had been posted to foot duty at Croydon, still awaiting the promised engagement ring that had accompanied his proposal of marriage, following their first moment of sexual union under the gymnasium boxing ring. She'd been a stupid cow to let herself think he would actually do it. But yet she had believed him. He was young and educated and once he'd shaken off his neo-puritan hang ups he'd gotten his lips round a nice bit of juicy meat like a real man. A man destined for commissioner and a lifetime of Common Purpose seminars couldn't take with him a girl with a tattooed potato plant growing out of her furrow with Maris Piper roots and spuds all down her thighs.

She closed her eyes. If she could find that sodding ferret, she could change her life and need no one. She was thirty-five, alone and still a full blooded blue-eyed blonde woman. But time was running out. She thought back to her youth, when she'd left school to be an actress. She'd done well at drama college. She remembered the guy from there whose face she thought she'd seen in the crowd on TV. He'd given her a knee trembler in the bog at a slam poetry festival. What was his fucking name? Idly she answered her mobile.

"Yup?"

She could only hear something like a sigh.

"Speak or fuck off."

"Selena – it's Crispin Bissel. I need you."

She sat up. Her friend Rita had read something like this in the tarot cards last week.

"You've bought my ring and you're craving my forgiveness and woman love?"

She listened to more sighs.

"OK – I forgive you. What the fuck do you want?"

In the silence she had to acknowledge she was intrigued and slightly aroused. Deep down he was a sexy naughty boy. His guilt and embarrassment were a turn on and a challenge to a woman who liked to dominate.

"Selena, I need a good-looking eye-candy woman to put in front of the cameras. I want you to front up the south London sewer squad and start the search for Frankie Ferret. I couldn't believe my luck when I saw you on the personnel list at Croydon."

"So, you want me up to my neck in shit down some drain?"

"No, you just have to pose, smile and you know –,"

"What? Get my pussy out and see if the ferret can't resist a scurry up my vagina."

"Selena – you know I care about you. I care about your integrity, dignity and holistic entity as a being."

"But you'd never troubled to know where I was. I'm guessing in that case you don't want to fuck me and then marry me like you said?"

"I do, you know...but in the context of a wider interpersonal nexus."

"You just want to fuck me first and then put me down a drain."

"I want you to help me but also save Christmas for a world of children. Where there is despair, you can bring hope. Where there is anguish you can bring the balm of your beauty. It's your chance to be a celebrity."

Selena thought for a moment.

"I'm on shift a ten o' clock. Get yourself down here with a meat feast pizza and let me look you in the eyes. If not, you can fuck off."

"Text me your address. I'll land on the police station roof in the chopper. We won't regret this."

4 CHAPTER FOUR

Crispin Bissel put down his phone. Talking to Selena Fontesse had stirred wonderful memories. OK, she was a tattooed mature ex-webcam girl, but every joy of his life was wrapped around the memory of her. She'd force-fed him his first pork pie wrapped in her moistened panties as an act of the sexual domination he craved. She'd spread Bovril on his genitals and then eaten it off buttered croissants, making him watch. He'd fucked her and kissed her lips. He'd been a virgin, only ever having known the warmth of intercourse via a hole in a microwaved melon. He'd longed for her, had wanted to marry her but a man in his position would never be free. Every tweet, every Facebook comment, every school playground word, every ex-girlfriend, every public-school wank-off of a friend in need could be used against an ambitious man by bitter rivals. The elite classes hugged and cried in victim groups for public consumption, but Crispin Bissel had learned enough from police work to see the dark stain of jealousy and treachery in the heart of man. As he reflected on Selena, he knew that she was his Achilles heel slithering on an organic banana skin. Strangely he felt safe with her. She would never know it, but he loved her. The denial of the joy of her to himself was his greatest self-loathing pleasure.

The Metropolitan Police chopper, call sign India Nine Nine, hovered over the roof of Croydon police station, navigation lights off.

"Fucking jump then," yelled the pilot.

"Can't you land?"

"Yeah but there's climate cataclysm demonstrators tracking us for carbon emissions. I can't land without lights."

Crispin leapt into the darkness. He hit the ground hard, turning over his ankle. That was all he needed. A uniformed police inspector stepped forward.

"Nice of you to drop in, sir. We've got a stuffed-crust meat feast and a Texas meat meltdown in the car along with two bottles of *vino rosso*. I believe you wish to encounter Constable Fontesse at her abode." The officer spoke in a staccato police official style.

"Yes, that would be fantastic."

"And a fantastic taste in the double X chromosome binary gender format if I may say so, sir. It is rumoured you may be seeking officers as celebrity presenters…,"

Chief Inspector Bissel wondered if anything was secure in the police system. He also longed for the past when you could openly just say words like *female*.

"Could be… why do you ask?"

"I have media experience and exposure myself. Just this morning I led the crowd of morons with their fake ferrets and white vans for Julian Gooseganda, the BBC producer."

"Was all that a set up?"

"I just followed orders, sir. I organised some off-duty colleagues and the film crew had a few bods. So, if you needed a celebrity male angle… my wife would be very proud, sir."

"I'll keep you in mind."

The patrol car turned off its blue lights and sirens as it drew up in a quiet residential street. Large houses displayed a faded multi-occupied languid exhaustion and the noble laurel bush squalor of urban litter. Crispin stepped from the vehicle with the wine and pizzas. The front door swung open as he limped on his swelling ankle. And there she stood, smiling, wearing a tight-fitting top and mini skirt with a pattern of halved figs and rigid courgettes. An aching surge gripped his loins. There'd been no release for a year.

"Selena –,"

He wanted to say he loved her. He would have opened his arms had it not been for the pizza boxes and carrier bag.

He closed his eyes as her arms folded around him. He felt the melting softness of her breasts, her hand on his ass pulling him to her.

"I hope you're still a naughty boy Crispin?"

Now he was fighting not to spend his man force against the warm pizza box containing his Texas meat meltdown.

"It's so good to see you. You look so much the part. The cameras will eat you."

"I was hoping for something more naughty than a camera."

Every time she pronounced the word *naughty*, pushing her soft lips forward, letting her wet pink tongue almost *click* the 'T' sound on the roof of her warm mouth, he had to gulp. When she let her blue eyes soften holding his gaze, parting her lips, trailing a soft hand down his cheek, he could do nothing but sigh.

"Naughty, naughty boy, Crispin. I hope you've got some hot meat for me? Come on – I've got to get to work tonight."

He followed her up the wide threadbare carpeted stair, still equipped with old fashioned stair rods. The ambiance of the house took him back to the bourgeois home where he'd lived as son of a university professor and his member of European parliament mother. Could he ever introduce them to Selena Fontesse? He knew the answer.

Since Bert Brickstone had snaffled his lunch, Crispin ate hungrily. Selena did the same swigging the wine and starting on the second bottle. He knew he'd never been happier than he was now to be with her. It had been a year since he'd seen her. She did look a little older, around the eyes and mouth. Maybe she'd gained a few pounds. It didn't alter her soft loveliness. In front of the cameras she would be a star and men, other hard ruthless terrifying men, would desire her. He felt a sharp stab of jealousy.

"You don't have to work tonight Selena. I'm putting you in front of the press at ten o'clock in the morning. I want you over the open manhole where Frankie was last seen. Can you do tears? Do you have a child or something and could feel their pain?"

"You know I've not got a child. The selfish prick who said he'd marry me ditched me to go back to shooting his load into hot melons."

Crispin ignored her aura of hostility. He needed her on his side.

"A nephew, niece, god child."

"Yeah, I've got a sister with a brat. She's a slag and the kid's got hyperactive smack in the gob disorder."

"Selena – I love your humour but if you could introduce the concept of this traumatized child... a child imprinted with your own beautiful blood."

"Fuck off – the kid's a shit."

Crispin held his face with his hands.

"Selena please – you trained as an actress; you are on the eve of stardom."

She smiled at him.

"OK, I feel his pain and I know I hold the innocent hearts of angels as I descend into the sewers. How does that sound?"

"Well, don't overplay it. What we need is sincerity with

competence. We need the warm breasts of a beautiful woman where a nation can unite to cry out their grief. I need you to offer a wounded people a cleavage of comfort allied to the ruthless steel of female courage."

"Fucking hell Crispin – that level of stuff is above my pay grade. Here's the deal. We finish the wine, you sleep in my arms and let me know again the passion of your lust and need for me. Then, after a full Wetherspoon's breakfast, as your treat, we do the press conference. Then you give in to the person you really are and marry me by special license."

He slugged back the dregs of the second bottle of wine, watching Selena undress. The womanly spill and swell of her belly was a joy. There was a perfection of cellulite that made him long for her imperfection. He needed the taste of her. He pulled off his uniform, cursing the wine and the brewer's droop afflicting his penis. She stretched out on the bed exposing her open loveliness. His desire and tongue homed in on her tattooed potato plant.

"Deal or no deal?" she said, holding him by his hair poised above her mound of Maris.

"Deal. Deal, deal, deal, my angel," he said as she held his tongue above her furrow."

She dropped the plough share of his desire into her fertile soil. He abandoned himself to the rich tilth of her surrender.

The phone was ringing in Downing street. It was 3am. Prime Minister Basil Montacute-Jones sighed as he replaced the stopper of his crystal decanter of cognac. A young assistant took the call and handed Basil the receiver.

"It's the commissioner of police, sir."

The PM rolled his eyes and unstopped the brandy, pouring himself a generous ration. He muttered unrepeatable remarks about female sexuality. Iona Peniston had not been a favourite since an unfortunate incident with one of his housemaids.

"Commissioner – how nice. Any ferret news?"

"Only tangentially. We went to arrest the courier van driver and found him tied up under a tarpaulin in the garden of his squalid dwelling in Dagenham. Some thugs wearing Viktor Pinupskin T-shirts and Cossack hats attacked him and stole his van and identity documents. He'd been there for three days."

"So, it was the Russians."

"It might be a double bluff, sir. I mean, they seemed to be wanting us to know that. Anyone can dress up as a Russian."

"Triple bluff is an old KGB tactic. Didn't you see the *Babushkas* driving the tanks into Crimea claiming they were on their way to the Eurovision song contest? I knew Pinupskin was behind this. Ever since he started posing with kittens on his calendars MI5 had been briefing something was going on. OK, full COBRA meeting in the underground war rooms as soon as you can get here."

The PM threw back the cognac. He flapped a hand impatiently at the young aide.

"Get the codes for the nukes and alert the Americans. Then make up some sandwiches – mine's a rare beef and English mustard. Any leftie types and that ghastly queer at the ministry of stinking fish get cheese, OK?"

The prime minister stood and went to the imposing sideboard. He picked up a large box of Havana cigars, raised two fingers to himself in the gilt framed mirror and headed for the lift.

The air extraction fans hummed in the underground bunker. A wall had been covered with a map of the Croydon sewer network. Everyone turned to one man, Dickon Maltravers, Head of Intelligence.

"OK. We believe we were right. A few hours after the incident we began to see bots on social media. Some are promoting a cuddly toy Russian bear with the features of Viktor Pinupskin. Other sites are pushing out propaganda for a referendum to choose a replacement for Frankie Ferret. Small crowds are already beginning to develop around parliament. The nation is divided. The Russians have offered the BBC a genetically modified orphaned pygmy brown bear cub. This is the new style of imperialism. We're blocking all images, but Russian propaganda TV is pumping it out. The sight of that baby bear will rip into the hearts of a nation already distraught with grief. If the nation wants that orphaned baby bear, they'll string up any politician standing in their way."

"Well, we did do it to them with 60's pop music," said the young minister for culture.

The PM nodded.

"True – that's how potent this cultural imperialism shit is. So, what are we doing, Dickon?"

"It looks like this referendum movement is unstoppable. We can't just tell the people they're thick morons being manipulated by the Russians. The Scottish Nationalists want a Highland stag, a sturgeon or a salmon on the ballot paper. We've started feeding the media images of ignorant mobs to show that the common people can't be trusted to make the complex choices. We've got insiders in most places to keep that as the editorial line."

The PM groaned, raking his hand through his wild grey curls.

"Jesus Christ. Just tell me why this bloody bear is an orphan. I suppose Viktor killed its parents to make a posing rug for his photo shoots.?"

"It was born in a test tube, sir. There's a suggestion that – you know – the sperm, was from a human donor."

"Pinupskin?"

For a moment the room seemed to stop in a horrified silence.

"Agents are saying that, sir. We're trying to get some DNA, but the face does bear a certain similarity. There's rumours it can speak."

The head of intelligence opened his briefcase and distributed some grainy long lens shots of a Russian army convoy, a soldier in the turret of an armoured personnel carrier, cradling a bear cub in his arms.

The PM stared at the image. There was no doubt. Idly he placed a cigar between his lips.

"So, if Pinupskin can do it, what's stopping us from doing it?"

"Morals maybe, sir?" said Dame Iona Peniston.

"Fuck off you self-righteous old bag," said the PM. "I've got a better idea. Let's use a panda – symbolic of that yin yang bollocks. Fucking things don't want to breed with other pandas anyway. It'd be symbolic of black and white living in perfect harmony. It'll bond us with the Chinese, unite society and scoop a massive market. Get some scientists lined up and crack on with it."

"Are you serious, sir?" asked Jacob Goldstein, chief secretary to the treasury.

"Of course I'm serious. I'm a big-plan man, a man with vision. Tell me when the egg is ready and I'll get you some of my little spermy tadpoles."

"And what about Frankie?"

"Pull out all the stops. Even dead there might be the chance of cloning him. Just remember, I'm a man of the people. We are not a self-seeking cynical elite. We must show we are with the lumpen prols, crying their tears, feeling their low information shallow sentimentality and loving their tasteless talent shows. Can we get any half alive politico on to that TV dancing show next week? Find someone and make them a lord or something."

"Now you are being stupid," commented Dame Iona Peniston.

6 CHAPTER SIX

In the first light of a winter dawn, Selena pressed her lips against Crispin's back. An hour earlier his liver and kidneys had processed enough alcohol out of his body to cure his brewer's droop. Once again, they had been united in the fullness of reckless love. It was 6am and there was a world to be faced. Passion had made her hungry.

"Wetherspoon's opens at seven," she whispered.

"I can't – I came in uniform. If anyone saw me in there munching bacon and sausage with fried egg there'd be an outrage among my Twitter followers."

Reciting the words of the menu made him yearn for the fullest ever, full English breakfast. He got up and found the bathroom. The shower cleared his mind. *He'd agreed to marry Selena.* For sure it had been under duress, but he had said it was a deal. He set aside all other concerns and thought of her. He would have a life of unbridled sexual passion. He would have black pudding and crispy bacon washed down with tea made with milk. He was just twenty-four and she would soon be thirty-six. Emmanuel Macron had shagged his far older teacher from school, married her and had still become a multi-millionaire and president of France. Macron had never posted pictures of his vegan meals on Instagram. A thing like that defined the bars of a man's cage.

Selena wandered in to the bathroom and squatted noisily on the toilet.

"Ooh, dear me, *windypops*," she remarked.

"God, Selena," he gasped.

"Only a love-puff, *Crispyducks*. We're together now, we've got to embrace intimacy."

A wave of horror and revulsion rolled through his soul. He'd never seen her or any woman this close up. His head swam.

"I've got the press at Croydon nick for ten o'clock. We need to run through some ideas of what you're going to say. I'll do the serious management angles."

"Is that cos I'm too thick?"

"It's because you're not a Chief Inspector from the media hub."

"'Oity toity la-di-da to you then. You forget I used to ad lib my way through sex with a parsnip. They can talk dirty but they're famously poor at conversation."

"Selena – don't be difficult please."

"Well how about 'good morning my gorgeous sweet lover'. How about a kiss and a 'can't wait until I've made you mine'?"

"Yes, well of course all of that. First we've got to prepare for the press conference."

He knew there was no hope of distracting her. He'd made a deal and she was going to close it.

"OK *Crispyducks* – talk to me over breakfast at Wetherspoon's. I'm going to have a right good blow out with mushers and beans."

"Selena – you know I'm a vegan. Calling me *Crispyducks* is quite bruising, almost wounding."

"Fucking snowflake you are. I'm only having some fun.

Let's go!"

There was no way he could go to a pub in full police uniform. If someone recognized him, he'd be finished. He knew that if he smelled cooking bacon he'd be lost.

"I can't Selena, I've got no casual clothes and it's against police regulations to wear part-uniform."

She smiled and held his sack in her hand. She squeezed just enough to elicit more pain than pleasure.

"My sweet, sweet lover man, I've thought of all that. I've set out some of my clothes to wear. We're going as girlie lovers. I kind of like that kink, don't you? You're quite fair skinned so use my leg razor on your chops. Believe me no one will recognize you. Once we're married, we can do all sorts together."

He stared at her. He had to keep her onside. He'd done all the courses on tolerance and equality. He dare not show any prejudice towards cross-dressers or gay lovers. If it meant he could escape recognition, keep her sweet and brief her for the press conference, it was his duty to go through with it. At police training school one of the instructors had told the class that one day every cop is tested to his limits and to be ready. His day had come. He dressed in a red, knee-length long-sleeved dress and threw an artistic silky scarf around his neck. Shoes? What the fuck could he do with his size eleven feet? As he pondered, Selena came from her shower and applied his lip gloss, eye shadow and false lashes.

"Why the fuck do I need all this make-up?"

"If I'm a lezzer I'm not being seen with a gronk. I've got my standards *Crispyducks*. Take a look in the mirror – I reckon you'll pull in the boozer."

He checked his look. Truth to tell he *was* pretty. Her hold-up lace topped stockings were smooth as he crossed his legs. Her silky panties felt sexy against his manhood which twitched with a little ping. All the lecturers at Oxford had stated the fluidity of gender. What it was to be an educated man. She handed him a pair of size six sequined flip flop sandals.

"Your feet will just have to overhang. All that matters is the sparkle from the straps. Come on – we need to get a move on. Put your wallet in that shoulder bag and walk the walk."

They stepped out into the dawn washed streets of Croydon. It was that time of stretching shop front clatter, the last shreds of night fleeing the street cleaner's merciless advancing brush of time. He'd linked arms with Selena as he shortened his stride to keep in step. Was he elevating his pitch of voice a little? He dared not admit it but this little walk on the wild side was… you know, wild.

Selena stopped a friendly looking postie who was staring at a large heavy manhole cover.

"'Ere mate – can you do us a photo on my mobile. We're getting married later."

He answered in a gruff but kind voice. He was the type of man who liked to chat.

"Sure, I mean normal life has to go on don't it. I thought I'd heard a squeak down there. Must have been a car fan belt or summink. It's a million quid if you find Frankie. My grandkids are in bits and the wife ain't too good. She was bad with Diana, but this is worse. They've started laying flowers and messages down at the shopping mall."

The guy snapped a couple of shots and handed back the phone.

"Bloody good luck darlin'. I'll give you lovely girls a kiss for luck."

The postie planted a cigarette-flavoured wet kiss on Crispin's cheek. He moved on to Selena and looked ready for another round.

"Thanks mate," said Crispin in his deepest voice, moving

away. "Jesus Selena, don't push your luck."

"Now you know what it's like to be a girl in the testosterone-driven jungle of the patriarchs," she replied, linking his arm.

He nodded. He was learning things. He knew that by now his digital image would be on some photo library in the cloud. He was afloat but a heavily-armed submarine had him in the cross hairs of its periscope. Somehow it didn't seem so bad to be destroyed at the hands of a woman he loved.

Selena knew she was being a bitch. She'd dressed him up and had the shots on her phone. He'd agreed to the marriage deal, but she knew she needed more than his word alone. Secretly she'd snapped him a couple of times with his Texas meat meltdown. Getting him in drag munching a full English sausage would be the nuclear option. And it was all because she loved him. She was sure he would never love her, but he was too young and wet to understand love. A man like him had to eat love from a nosebag while she sat on his back with a whip. She was his only chance of expressing himself on the Earth. He was her only chance of finding the right type of naughty boy to submit to her need to educate. She would prefer a submission, but now she had the punch to win by a knockout.

They had arrived at Wetherspoon's in George Street Croydon. She went to the bar and placed orders, holding out her hand to Crispin for cash. He fumbled for pockets.

"Try your handbag *Crispyducks*," she purred, winking at the bar man.

Chief Inspector Bissel looked up to see the young guy's eyes warmly on his as he handed over the note.

"That's perfect sweetie. I always say it's so nice to have

someone new at breakfast," he said.

Crispin's mind buzzed. He didn't mind being fluid with Selena, but he'd never mastered swimming freestyle. After today, he'd stick to breaststroke.

They waited for their meals and swigged tea. He needed her to focus on her mission.

"Now, you're going to be Sergeant Fontesse. The public see rank as a badge of being in control and intelligence. You need to show emotion and caring. Remember that poor postie with his tear-stained family. Tell the folks how that meeting touched your heart. We care but we're tough. Hope may be fading but you believe –,"

"I get it Crispin. I went to acting school remember. Do you want cleavage, doe-eyed wistful longing or both?"

"Can you do both?"

"Sure, just tell the camera to be ready for a flash. As I do the over the shoulder misty eyes, he needs to slip down to my open blouse. I'll let my tunic flap aside."

A plate arrived hot from paradise. Crispin went straight for the pork sausage. The universe screamed like the Munch painting. His heart raced but settled as he ate a righteous hash brown. Sin, sin. Was there any joy outside of sin?

"So, after the shoot, we can close the deal as agreed," she said.

He took a quick breath and looked into her clear blue eyes.

"Yes, yes of course."

"You're so romantic *Crispyducks*."

He didn't respond, merely smiling weakly as she took a few more snaps. He just had to get her through the conference. Then he could dump her and run. Or maybe not?

The bar had become noisy. Builders gobbled through great plates of cholesterol. A crowd of loud Hooray types in tight beige stripy jumpers and designer jeans had swarmed in. Crispin's heart sank to see one of them had a microphone. These were posho media types. An anorexic looking woman was starting a live vox pop on the Frankie situation for the ITV breakfast show. His bladder was bursting from the Wetherspoon's infinite refills of tea. He dashed to the toilets and stood at a urinal. Suddenly he realised he had no trouser fly zip. He had no trousers. He glanced behind him at the cubicles, but they were all occupied by clients releasing their bowels with groans, squirts, plops and farts. His flow had started so he had to press on, lifting the red satin dress and praying he could finish before anyone discovered him.

The entrance door swung open. Footsteps approached from behind. A man stood at the adjoining stall even though others were vacant. Crispin stared at the wall, affecting a fascination with plastic sanitary joints. He dared not look at his impromptu neighbour. A voice, he recognised that voice.

"I knew you media-types were bloody fairies but it's a bit early for me mate," said Superintendent Bert Brickstone.

Crispin looked away. If he'd been a spy the authorities would have issued him a cyanide suicide pill for this type of situation. His boss continued.

"Mind you, I'm not one to judge. A standing prick knows no conscience and I saw a few ladyboys when I was a young sailor in the Royal Navy. You get to a certain point and you just say fuck it and get on cos usually you've already paid up. Made a bloody man of me you know."

Maybe it would be better to respond. He was aware that Bert was leaning towards him to get a better look at the plumbing.

"Yes, the navy offers great opportunities," said Crispin.

"That it does boy, when you've got a stiffy and a big matelot's hand slides into your hammock you ain't got to worry about who's on the end of it."

Strong fingers squeezed Crispin's ass cheek as his companion pulled in and re-zipped. The shock made him drop the hem of his dress as his flow soaked the fabric. He heard Bert at the door.

"Live and let live I say. Nice ass, not bad legs boy. If I was you, I'd have a trim – you know…?"

The door closed. Fuck. Fuck. Fuck. There was no way he could go back out into the bar. Piss was dripping off his dress onto his sequined-sandaled-feet, and he could not risk anyone recognising him, most of all Bert Brickstone. There was only the window which opened outwards and only with a small gap. He just had to try.

Selena Fontesse was growing impatient. It was 8:30am and she had to get ready for her appointment with fame. She idly watched a make-up girl dropping glycerine tears onto the cheeks of a young scaffolder who'd volunteered to be interviewed about Frankie Ferret by a CNN reporter. Where the fuck was Crispin? Where indeed? She knew he wasn't going to claim her as his bride. Deep down she'd always known. She'd never blackmail or humiliate him but at least she had the stuff to give him a fright. She wouldn't do it for the best and worst of reasons. She loved him.

She stood up, checked the bar, collected Crispin's handbag and walked out. Obviously, he'd run away and if there was a tear in her eye it wasn't so much sorrow as disappointment and anger at herself. A large fire engine was making its way through the traffic. A complete window frame and glass littered the pavement and road. A crowd of public and media were looking up at the building. A woman was calling kindly into the sky.

"My friend, I am a trained counsellor. Hold on. We all share your pain. Frankie may be alive. Don't jump while there is still hope."

A BBC legend, Jonathan Dingleberry, exhumed because of the emergency, was addressing the nation live in hushed sad tones.

"This is the reality of a proud people ennobled by sorrow. A nation once divided by politics but united in grief. A poor young girl broke down in the bar. She came to Croydon with her friends who are here behind me. They laid flowers at the poignant shrine in the shopping mall and it was there that this poor girl became overwhelmed."

Dingleberry swept his hand behind him to indicate a posse of wailing teenagers who still managed to pout and wave at the cameras.

Selena glanced up. Yes, the figure clinging to the window ledge and wearing her red dress was Crispin Bissel. The bastard must have been so desperate to escape. She watched as firemen swung an escape ladder into position and a brawny hero threw the would-be suicide over his shoulder. The crowd applauded. Dingleberry waited at the base of the ladder and thrust the mic' under Fireman Sam's nose.

"Do you feel there is a sense in which your heroism has brought a moment of hope to a nation in torment," he said.

"Yeah well, this fucking tranny is soaked in piss, so you'd better stand back mate," said the hero.

The instant Crispin was released he ran. No hesitation, wild and mindless, flat out, no looking back. He ran and ran and ran. His residual reptilian brain wiped out one of the world's finest educations in a zillionth of a millisecond. Now he knew blind animal terror. Life was a learning curve ball.

8 CHAPTER EIGHT

As she searched for her key, Crispin emerged from behind the trash bins at one side of the front garden.

"You bastard. You bastard," she said.

"I can explain. I wet myself when my boss goosed me."

"So *Crispyducks*, you leave your future wife deserted without even a phone call."

"My phone is my handbag. I tried to force myself through the window, but the frame gave way."

A moment of hope, that was true, he didn't have his phone.

"So, you do love me. We are getting married?"

"Yes. Yes, but I need my uniform and to get to the press conference."

"I don't believe you. Get your stuff for now and we'll talk after the media-fest. I don't really want you in my sight."

The last thing Crispin wanted was a long conversation about his nuptials. He pulled off his wet clothes and left them in the bath. He threw on his uniform and spoke to her from the door.

"I'm sorry Selena. I can explain. I'll see you at the police station at 0945. I can tell you're angry with me but just see this as your chance in life. We want emotion, caring and cleavage, OK?”

“And then you want to make me yours for the rest of our lives, *you lying prick.*”

He couldn’t frame any kind of answer he could see as helpful. He put back his shoulders and strode away. His life was back on track. Within a few minutes he was picking his way across cables and film equipment trailing from an array of satellite trucks. At the police station rear entrance there was a scrum of famous correspondents, assistant political editors, deputy editors, assistant deputy editors and Lindsay Garricker, the ex-England centre forward who was seated on a portable throne and receiving a foot manicure while eating a bag of crisps. He saw the political queen of political correspondents Sophia Crest heading for him. She stared and exchanged glances with a wispy young guy crawling at her feet with a furry microphone on a stick. She seemed to be hesitating. Crispin pushed out his chest and smiled.

“Hey, Sophia, I didn’t know I was this important,” he quipped.

“You’re not. Remind me who you are.”

“Chief Inspector Crispin Bissel. I’m the *ferret loving public face of the filth.*”

“Are you sure you’re OK to speak? We can go for a world exclusive if you think you’re ready?”

“Sure, we’re pros you and me.”

Ms Crest glanced back at her producer who shrugged.

“We’ve networked to just about everyone Sofe, so yah, if the guy’s cool it’s all good TV. We’re just coming out of a commercial for ferret tampons, so the mood is set. I’ll count you in Sofie baby.”

Crispin watched him raising his fingers as he set up the cue. She gave him a last bizarre troubled glance, took her foot crossover high-heeled media stance and smiled into camera with her beautiful radiating intelligence.

"Good morning from Croydon. We have with us Chief Inspector Crispin Bissel who is heading the search for Frankie Ferret. Everyone just wants to know if there's any progress. Can you comment on the Russian involvement?"

"Thank you, Sophia. You know even street hardened cops are feeling the pain of the nation. Just this morning a beautiful young girl tried to end it all only a few streets from here. My fiancée has family broken by these events. I feel the weight of grief and carry that passion into my work. You know Frankie was the true people's prince of ferrets."

He judged it was now time to show his sincerity. He raised his hands to his face. Brushing on the inside skin of his fingers were the bristles of his false lashes. He was still in full fem make-up including scarlet lip gloss. He could hear the beautiful Ms Crest stifling a giggle. He pulled his hands away. He had to fight on.

"And the Metropolitan Police represents all genders and orientations. In this time of sorrow, we need to show that sincerely to all communities."

"Oh wow – Crispin, so you're reaching out, showing that love trumps hate, showing that all men are brothers in a nexus of fluid unity."

"That is how we all see it at Scotland Yard, Sophia. And that's how Frankie would have wanted us to remember him – if he were dead of course."

"That's so beautiful Crispin. And Frankie's message of inclusion is what you're proclaiming in your own person," cooed Sophia Crest.

"Yes, actions are worth more than words."

Crispin became aware that armies of media types had formed an applauding crowd. Someone was waving a Ferret Pride placard.

"Thank you so much, Chief Inspector. You've shared something very valuable with us today. OK, we'll let the police get on with their work and turn to events in Westminster. The Russian ambassador has been called to the Foreign Office –,"

Crispin strode away, his head high. He had carved out a place for himself in history. Only one thing worried him. What the fuck was a nexus of fluid unity? In his new status it was the kind of thing he'd have to know.

Selena had seen the scrum at the back gate and had entered the police station via the front entrance. Behind the counter she could see and hear an apoplectic middle-aged man assailing the desk sergeant.

"That cunt is out there in full drag queen slap making us a laughing stock. Can't you just throw a master switch and cut them off?" bellowed Bert Brickstone.

She went to the back door and looked across the yard to where Crispin was raw meat in a feeding frenzy of luvvies. Jesus, a male Chief Inspector in full make-up. He really was quite pretty. A few feet away a Sky News anchor man was hamming it up to camera.

"It's really something when a man reaches out to our community of splintered communities by openly touching himself…,"

"Miss Fontesse?" came a soft voice.

She turned to see a young TV production assistant.

"Yes."

"We need to dust your face and maybe shadow your cleavage a little. Mammary sweat under the lights can take out the definition – you know the lewd male focus area."

"Do all the presenters enhance their lewd male focus areas?"

"I can't talk about things like that. It's their private data and it has to be protected."

"Might it be easier if I just kept my private data

protected?”

“Oh no, big data is everything these days and your chief – wots-her-name – Dame Iona Peniston, has asked for them.”

“Sure, *enhance me to the end of love*, sugar.”

“Pardon me?”

“I’m guessing you don’t do Leonard Cohen?”

“I think my nan did.”

Selena sighed as the young woman enhanced her big data. She was probably old enough to be her nan at a stretch. She decided to chat.

“Have you been watching that cop out there with all the lashes and stuff?”

“Yeah, kind of a pretty thing isn’t he. Not my sort.”

“Really? Aren’t you young folk fluid and accepting?”

“On the surface but I want a dark dominator with abs and pecs. I need some tough tatts on him and maybe a matching one for me.”

Selena laughed.

“Avoid vegetables. It kinda typecasts a person.”

A few minutes later Selena found herself ushered to a makeshift studio. A guy in a frogman suit was holding a large German Shepherd dog which appeared attracted to her groin.

“Isn’t there supposed to be a dog handler too? asked Selena.

The frogman pulled aside his snorkel.

“I am the fuckin’ dog handler, the spending cuts mean we have to double up. Good job the mutt can swim.”

She set herself to calm and thought back to everything she’d learned at acting school. She ran her hands down over her big data, undid an extra button and gave her soul to the nation.

Time was a blur. Almost an hour later, the media had had

their fill. The assistant unpinned her mic'.

"God, you're a pro. You're double viral and three proposals of marriage, two from men. Not even Gretchen Thunderbird can do that helpless tear in the eye like you."

"She's a sweet religious kid on a mission. I'm a hard-bitten atheist trouper with a script."

"I won't tell anyone. I think you're special, very special."

With that the girl kissed her tenderly on the lips.

"I thought you wanted a stallion," said Selena.

"If it's a horse you can ride it," said the assistant as she picked up her tool bag and left.

Selena sat quietly in the film director's chair. She wasn't old but a world had grown up behind her that she just did not know or understand. She'd been wrong about missions. She had two. The first was to deal with *Crispyducks* Bissel once and for all. The second was to find Frankie Ferret. Those tears had not been fake. Those tears had been a badge of belonging, at last.

9 CHAPTER NINE

The Russian ambassador looked sheepish as Basil Montacute-Jones paced the Downing Street reception room around him, slamming his fist into the palm of the other hand.

"You fucking Ruskie cunts. Look I like Viktor, I'd even agreed to do a calendar shoot with him, you know guns and partridge kind of Christmas folksy. You send a bunch of *numpski* thugs over here to steal Frankie Ferret. The twats loaded up on vindaloo and have to stop for a shit in Croydon. Why?"

"Prime Minister, the Russian bowel is different. They thought no one would notice. The old Soviet guidebook said south London was a shithole. It was an old book and they're not linguists."

"Fuck. Fuck. Fuck. So they leave the van door open? It's only because a police dash cam saw it that we even know about it."

"Basil, please, they were desperate. You know how these things can be."

"Well, next time get some newer guidebooks in Russian. So why did Viktor want Frankie Ferret? I know all about his sex with polar bears or whatever. I trust we'll see it actually happening in his calendar?"

"Sir, ever since the innocent singing Babushkas were wrongly accused of invading Ukraine, your government has imposed sanctions – many against some very important sporting oilygarchs."

"You mean that footballing sugar daddy, Moron Molassovitch. I never did like the cut of his jib."

"The original plan was just to hold Frankie as a hostage, like the Iranian political model."

"Look, I know nobody goes into a negotiation without a no deal option. We all need a bit of leverage. It's no use falling out over a fucking elongated rat or whatever it is. The truth is it's united the nation. But hear me good Ivan Terribliski – any more stirring up referendums off-piste and stunts with baby bears and I'll kick your ass. I've got the fucking nuke codes somewhere here.

The PM made a show of searching his pockets.

"I'll pass on your diplomacy to the Kremlin, sir. President Viktor Pinupskin tends to drive policy you understand."

"Ivan, I do understand old son. Fucking dictators are a menace unless you want a decision about something. I'm a leader you see and the buck stops here. Listen, I'll make you an offer. I'll pass a motion for a referendum and campaign for the Russian bear. You lot get out of Ukraine after a glitzy summit between me and Viktor. I get the Nobel peace prize, a wedge of cash and my place in history. Oh – I'll want fifty-fifty on the bear merchandise."

The Russian ambassador reflected for a moment and fixed Basil Montacute-Jones with a firm gaze.

"Seventy thirty to Viktor and you might have a deal."

"I'll sleep on that one. Feel him out for me OK. Every extra ten percent you can get me, I'll cut you one percent."

"I can tell you were once a businessman, sir."

"Huh – sure not like those snowflake drongs down the

road. Look, there's a snivelling little politico from the Blubbering Demagogue party waiting outside. Send him in on your way out will you.

"Before I go Prime Minister, could Her Majesty's government push the referendum result the way we wanted?"

"Get out Ivan, this is a fucking *nudgeocracy*. That lot out there will toe the line believe me. Once the middle classes find out that bears are climate-endangered and that ferrets eat rabbits the game will be over. Nothing beats PC in the land of free thought. What a stupid question."

"What if Frankie did turn up?"

"Then I'm sure dear old Viktor would send some *numpskis* to deal with it. A few drops of Novichok somewhere in Croydon should do it. Ivan, the ferret is gone, dead. Trust me. Forget it."

The ambassador bowed as he exited the room, briefly acknowledging a short pale skinned man with a wispy beard in a cream suit and bow tie who was waiting in the hall.

"Well, get in here Blanchard, I've got a people to lead."

Kevin Blanchard gave a limp smile. As the country's most famous self-proclaimed flexigan, his career had never recovered from a tabloid shot of him munching a doner kebab on the way home from a Vote Romaine lettuce rally on his Westminster allotment. His voice was little more than a whisper.

"How can I help you, Prime Minister?"

"You know the situation with this bloody animal. It's our chance to unite the nation beyond the squalid yah-boo sucks stuff that makes you and me rich and famous. We have to face up to the fact that the creature is dead. I'm looking for a united approach to the future. If we go for a referendum, we need to shaft the Nationalists and that load of posho Trots, agreed?"

"We would need a policy conference, Prime Minister, the Liberal Demagogues are a consensual body."

"That's why you're a bunch of powerless nobodies. Look, Lord Blanchard of Chipping Sodbury, deputy prime minister, or whatever you want to be, with your votes and the government's, it's all over. HM gov' is going for the Pinupskin Bear cub."

"I've no connection with Chipping Sodbury, sir."

"Well choose your own title – Lord Doner of Kebab if you want."

Kevin Blanchard turned an even paler shade of beige and moved unsteadily to a chair.

"A cruel jibe, sir, if I may say –,"

"Look, sorry OK, I can't resist the Flashman parry-riposte."

"Maybe *Lord Legume*, sir, in recognition of my stance on Europe."

"Whatever. Now we have a deal, OK? Next thing I need a big favour from you. I believe you're in touch with Gretchen Thunderbird?"

"In what way, in touch?" asked Kevin Blanchard warily.

Basil expressed a sly smile on his fleshy face, knowing he'd cornered him.

"Like because your wife and nephew run her PR company."

Blanchard surrendered. The PM had only been flying a kite but had received a whisper from MI5 that an offshore trust "Amen 2 That" was funded by the Vatican bank and run by the Blanchards.

"I believe we could make contact."

"Right, for now we need to keep hope high and alive. Hope, yes hope is politics Kevin – Lord Legume I mean. Jam tomorrow postponed you understand? Now, there's a mass concert at Wembley on Sunday. That casting-couch lech,

Vandervel O'Brien, is directing it. Some piano guy – you know the one who does the royal grovelling stuff, he's re-written his song book with Frankie Ferret lyrics - Good-bye Frankie boy, Ferret in the bin, that kind of idea. There's going to be a mass cry-in, and the Red Barrows are doing a run-past up the pitch, tossing out red white and blue petals."

"Red Barrows, sir?"

"Yes – negative carbon – because of the climate loonies. They'll all be dressed up in pilot gear, so it'll seem authentic. I need you to get Gretchen Thunderbird there. I mean this is the big one Kev'. We keep hope alive until the crowd start waving their mobile phone lights and do a mass chorus of 'Goodbye Frankie boy'. I want Gretchen on the stage, you know, looking mad and visionary. She looks up into the night sky and sees a ring of fire and behind it is the constellation of the little bear, Ursa Minor. She falls down weeping and priests come in with video phones and clay tablets. She proclaims her vision and your PR company get the full copyright."

"Stone tablet, stage shows, audio book and music rights?"

"You've got it."

"It's a deal," said Lord Legume, extending a limp damp hand.

"Well fuck off and get on with it," said the PM waving him away and pulling out his mobile.

"Hey, Bro – get those containers unloaded and get the gear to Wembley for Sunday. I've got the army on standby to run street stalls. By midnight that bloody animal will be history like ninja turtles and action man dolls."

10 CHAPTER TEN

Chief Inspector Crispin Bissel had one vital mission before he left Croydon. A quick visit to Wetherspoon's and flash of his warrant card secured him the CCTV footage of all his time in the pub. One day he would check it out if he had to. All he knew of police work was training school and Mafia gangster films. Forty minutes later he slumped behind his desk in the Scotland Yard media hub. Whatever Selena had done with his eyelashes, one remained stuck as if with Super Glue. He needed to think and call his family. Shit, his mobile was still in that handbag in her Croydon bed-sit. At least she couldn't call him to make a wedding rendezvous. Every phone on every desk was ringing. Every officer was out with gangs of media *fameoids*. He picked up the receiver in front of him.

"Bissel."

"Darling it's Mummy. We're so, so proud of you. The Euro Parliament have been applauding your image on the screen for nearly an hour now. I'm calling Neil Flintlock later to see about getting you as a statue in Trafalgar Square. We're going to sing 'Ode to Joy' and then all go for a champagne dinner."

"So – you didn't mind the drag queen angle?"

"It's wonderful darling. It's inclusivity on acid. You were just so, so cool and proud."

Crispin thought for a moment. If his mother was prepared to accept him as possibly bi-sexual, maybe she could accept Selena?

"Did you see the girl, Sergeant Fontesse?"

"Oh yes. Awful, awful. Some of us were nearly sick. So common, so blowsy. Dreadful thing exposing her lewd male focus areas. Looked like she had a turnip tattoo."

"It's a sugar beet to show support for the Common Agricultural Policy."

"Bollocks Crispin, you made that up."

Quickly he thought back over everything that had happened, his night of love, the joy and freedom of being with her, a life encompassing a Wetherspoon's breakfast without guilt and torment. What were the true values of life? His hard-line manly boss had grabbed his ass and spoken honestly about the facts of life and pleasure. Words and attitudes were at best transient and at worst fake and deceitful. His mother wasn't quaffing champagne and singing the EU anthem because he'd been on world TV in drag. They were all acting out lies and fashion. He only knew what was in his heart.

"Mummy, I love her. I'm going to marry her."

All he heard on the line was a shriek, Germans bellowing Beethoven lyrics in the background and muffled foreign tongues.

"*Vite — elle est morte! Sie ist tot! Ma, non e morta —,*"

"Mummy, Mummy, I didn't mean it," he yelled into the phone.

"Darling, It's OK, I'm here. Don't joke with Mummy. The bubbles went up my nose."

"OK Mummy, have a nice evening."

He hung up. Well, he'd told her and now knew her

reaction. He needed to get to Selena and begin his real life.

"What the fuck?" said Bert Brickstone as he strolled in. "Either get that eyelash off or get the other one back on."

"I'm signalling bi-sexuality, sir."

"They're all fucking poofs to me boy. I've never seen a clown with one daft shoe."

"Sir, I need to get married."

"I always said you were a stupid twat but at least you're a man. Is she pregnant?"

"I don't think so. It's rather sexist to assume it's to a female, sir. Look, can I have the afternoon off?"

"You have to be joking young man. I've got orders to get you to the commissioner's office. Clear your desk. Dame Iona Peniston wants to keep you by her side as an aide from now on. You're the new face of inclusive law enforcement."

Crispin packed up his desk. Selena would understand. At least the photos of him were no longer a real threat. He could live through a greasy sausage-scandal if he had to. Oh Selena…

She lay back on her bed. She felt drained and empty. She felt like a foot trapped in an infinite fish pedicure. Right now, she should have been getting married. The bastard had just disappeared, like she knew he would. If only she could hate him, but she didn't have that type of mind. She called his number one more time. A phone was ringing. She tipped out the handbag she'd lent him. The twat had forgotten it when she'd more or less thrown him out still in his make-up. Now he was a superstar. It had been a mistake to use Super Glue on that eyelash. Maybe, maybe there was hope? He knew where to find her. Oh *Crispyducks…*

She phoned the police station.

"Sarge, I'll turn in for nights tonight as normal. I want to get back to a real life."

"Don't think that'll ever happen. There's press still outside and several dozen men have sent bouquets."

"I'll pick them up tonight and put them on the Frankie shrine in the mall."

"I'll put you on sewer duty. There's dozens of numpties trying to open drain covers to search for it and scoop the reward."

"Sounds perfect. I'm turning in and my phone will be off."

Dame Iona Peniston embraced Crispin with the strength of a wrestler.

"You've done well. Ever since I took this job there's been nothing but whingeing from trans-this and trans-that. Look, I know where I stand, and the world knows it. You have to remain ambiguous, maybe one day top and one day bottom if you see my drift."

"I was hoping to get married."

"What's his name?"

For a moment he considered chiding her for her blatant sexism.

"It's a woman ma'am."

"No, out of the question. Maybe once we're through this Ferret emergency. Maybe if she were ambiguous –,"

"I see."

"Crispin, you're on your way to the top. Everyone is so proud of you. Don't throw away this chance. Right, I'm flying to Madrid for a conference on counterfeit Manchego cheese. Foodies are *the* lobbyists. That turkey, Baron Twizzler, is creating a right old stink in the upper chamber and has demanded the boss. From now on I want you in the background for media continuity at all times. We'll be back tomorrow afternoon. There's my bag, pick it up. And fix that fucking eyelash."

Maybe he'd remembered her number wrongly. There was no response as if her phone was off. Maybe she'd topped herself in despair. There was no time to get another sim card and recover his directory. He'd tried several times from the office but now they were on their way to RAF Northolt for the government flight to Madrid. When you can do nothing, you just have to lie back and think of Selena. The convoy and outriders stopped outside a Boots Pharmacy to pick up some make-up and lashes. He added a tube of Super Glue in case he couldn't re-apply a new set. Three women approached for autographs and selfies. Perhaps he wouldn't be famous in Madrid.

Police Constable Selena Fontesse paraded for night duty with the troops on red shift. The instant she'd finished her media show, she'd handed in her sergeant's chevrons. She only had one year's service and she felt like a fake. She was a fake. She'd looked into the toilet bowl of fame and had thrown up. All the same she'd chosen to wear a skirt and stockings with suspenders on the advice of the media hub. Before she could start her proper foot patrol in central

Croydon, she had to donate all her fan-mail bouquets to Frankie's shrine in the Whitgift mall. She'd done some over the shoulder doe-eyed stuff and a slight tease of lewd male focus area for the press core on the promise that they would then go home. The reporter from the Sun had cheekily hidden behind a market stall, popping out to beg for an exclusive single rose-laying with teasy suspender, sad-faced princess pose. At last she was free. She'd given a good account of herself in a pub fight, run to a car up a lamppost with blood and fractures and scooped up a poor junkie girl shivering in a doorway begging for a fix. God, it was so good to back in the flow of life. She ate a cheese sandwich at 3am with an old-sweat patrol car driver. He had that thousand-yard stare and memories of the old days with proper car chases and fist fights with hard men. She knew she'd be all over the morning papers but then it would all fade and she'd be alone. She'd be that slightly distanced woman who'd been on tele, maybe won a daytime quiz or done a talent show. Oh, fuck you, *Crispyducks*.

It was about 4am, policeman time, when the trucks fall off the road, when the old hearts stop, when the cockerels feel the first hints of mortality. This was slack water time. A space that didn't exist like the spring day you would hold forever, like the first time you touch a baby's hand and it grips, a space without being when time sits back, draws breath and feels the weight of life in its palm, knowing that soon it will have to make that fist and fight again. Love had put a poetry in her heart. Oh, fuck you, *Crispyducks*.

She wandered idly down Wellesley Road, towards the Lunar House UK Immigration Headquarters building. A grief counselling bus parked on the forecourt was still accepting a few stragglers.

A newspaper van swept past; her shoulder radio had gone quiet. There was nothing. Nothing. She'd learned that ferrets are crepuscular and are active at dusk and dawn. She had also learned that they often went into a "dead sleep" where they could almost seem exactly that – dead. A shoelace was undone, and she bent to re-tie it. Then something distracted her.

"Cheep. Mmmmmmcheep."

She stopped, there was a sound from under a grilled manhole cover. She could just see down into a deep drain, like a well with a ladder bolted to the wall. She listened again. There was no one in sight so she bent down, placing her ear to the cover. Deep below water was running. She saw the scurry of a rat.

"Cheep. *Mmmmmmcheep*."

The cover was heavy, and she had no tools. She stayed in position, ear to the metal. She heard a vehicle on the road behind her. The tyres squealed as it pulled up. The engine was rumbly and powerful.

"I look all my life in all the world for my shooting star. At last in *magnifica Londra,* I find a rising moon. Hey, *bella mia* – 'ow I 'elp a beautiful woman like a you?"

She squinted behind her. To the source of the deep musical voice. In the distance was a Ferrari. Above her was Carlo *Love-God* di Rigatoni, straight out of her stallion romance. He wore a kingfisher-blue suit and sported an immaculately trimmed fashion beard. His shirt was a slim fit and brilliant against his tanned skin. Only the whiteness of his perfect teeth outshone the lustre of his clothing. A waft of pungent aftershave struck her senses.

"Hmm, is that 'The One' by Dolce and Portakabin?" she asked.

"*Si, perfetto*. I am 'The One.'"

"Well, have you got a jack handle or any tool in that thing?"

"I don't know. Can you look?"

"What?"

"My look, my clothes, I can't touch grease."

"You're in the wrong place trying to pull me then mate. Where's the spare?"

"Spare?"

"*Si*, tyre – *puncturoni* – hiss hiss."

"*Ah capito*. The front I think."

She stood and brushed down her skirt. He was a good six feet four inches. He had only shoulders and deep dark eyes. He reached inside the car. The boot lid popped up. She spotted a wheel brace with a strong bladed end and grabbed it.

"This'll do. Come on." she ordered.

The stallion reared back from the sight of the tool.

"What a you do?"

"I'm going to get that cover up."

"Yes, this is an obvious plan for a beautiful woman with such eyes like the ocean in the Bay of *Napoli*, with hair like the golden fields of Tuscany."

She hesitated to tell him she was possibly on the trail of Frankie Ferret. She levered a crack in the cover and heaved aside the heavy metal.

"Do you want to help?"

"My suit, my look – I am worth ten thousand euros as I stand."

"Fuck off then."

"How can I. Those blue eyes, that blonde hair. I *wanta* you for mine for an eternity."

"So, you're going to ask a woman to go down a filthy drain with rats at the bottom while you stand there looking beautiful?"

"*Si*, here in *Londra* women are equal. When I get you to *Napoli* you will be worshiped like a queen."

"Christ, we've got enough of them here. Who does the

drains in *Napoli*?"

"*La Mafia*, they do everything but not too good."

"OK, hold my hat."

She took a deep breath and placed a foot on the ladder. She was going to get that million quid direct from Sir Brandon Pickell himself."

Looking up she could see the cold grey light of dawn getting fainter as she descended. She shone her police torch down into the darkness

"Cheep. *MmmmmCheep*."

It was closer now. She called out.

"Frankie, Frankie."

There was scurry as a mouse ran across her feet. She was in the rank gulley at the bottom of the shaft. She guessed she was thirty feet down. She felt a wave of panic and revulsion. Another mouse charged past as if it were being chased. Fuck – it was being chased.

"Frankie? Frankie is that you?"

"Amen," said Frankie.

She squatted down as he jumped onto her lap. At once he burrowed under her blouse and somehow twisted himself inside her bra and peeped his head out of her cleavage. A look of bliss and contentment spread across his adorable cute face. Within seconds he was asleep.

She had to think. This was a life changing moment. This animal was worth a cool million pounds. She had a duty to act as a police officer and regulations would prevent her from claiming the reward. If only she had her *Crispyducks*. If she had him, money would mean nothing. As it was, she had nothing. Nothing.

Wearily she climbed the ladder. On the second rung her foot twisted and her loose shoe fell away into the darkness. There was no way she was going back into a pit of rats with a bare foot. There was no need for stallion man to know she'd found him. He was still there as she hauled herself back out of the hole. Now she would have to bum a lift home.

"Nothing," she said.

"You were looking for that animal? Now your life begins. I am on my way to *Napoli*. I have a ferry to catch so this is your chance for a life with a man every woman would die to touch. I am Carlo di Rigatoni, the model, the face of a thousand dreams, the look of a hundred brands, the –,"

"The arrogance of a total prick," she added. "Look mate. Give me a lift round to my place. I need to pick something up for a friend before I come off shift."

It was a lie. If she could hide Frankie in a box or something, she would have time to think, maybe give her one last chance to contact Crispin. She didn't want to bend down with a ferret in her lewd male focus area. Everyone would think some bounty hunter had left the drain open. Carlo could give her a lift home; she could hide Frankie and then clock off shift as normal. It was perfect.

She slid into the seat of the Ferrari. He turned and flashed a knicker bursting stallion smile. His Latin nostrils flared with passion.

"You English beauties, you have the perfume of British musk. I understand but it is perhaps a little strong."

"It's called *Ferremone*," she said, only too aware of the pungent aroma of Frankie. She felt him nuzzle happily against her skin, sending up a wave of masculinity.

"Si, it is potent – how far to your place?"

"A few minutes, Carlo. Tell me about my blue eyes bouncing about on the bay of *Napoli*."

"*Si, che bellezza* you will bring. The *Napoli* girls are dark hairy jealous monsters."

"I see. I imagine you would marry me?"

"After a decent time and there are the wishes of *Mamma*.

I take my washing every week. She make a pasta *perfetta*. I put you in a house nearby and we make love on the golden sand at Posillipo."

"Nope, won't be any sand near my bits mate. Turn left here and pull up. Thanks for the ride."

The stallion flared his nostrils again.

"So, you will come with me to Italy?"

"To be frank, no. I can see you're a perfect romantic hero, but my heart is elsewhere."

"Then maybe you can thank me for my kindness with a kiss. This is your one chance to say you have known Carlo di Rigatoni."

She watched him unzipping his fly to expose his love machine.

"No thanks mate, I've only just had a cheese sandwich."

He reached out to pull her to his lips. She was aware of sensations she had never known before. There was a writhing and churning in her flesh like she'd read in all her romantic books. So, it was all true.

In a flash Frankie burst from her blouse and sank his teeth into the erect member of Carlo di Rigatoni. He let out a yell of pure panic and terror.

"He's a total carnivore mate and he's probably hungry."

She pulled out her phone snapping him and his exposed member.

"Frankie leave, come to Mummy," she said. The animal responded and burrowed back into her bra.

"Now – you fuck off and keep your trap shut. Any peep out of you the world sees these shots, OK?"

"*Si, si, si*. Get out my car you stinking bitch."

She took a few shots of the departing vehicle. Idly she stroked Frankie's head.

"Amen" he said.

Once inside she tried to get Frankie out of her cleavage.

Every time she pulled him out, he struggled and twisted back in. She had to go back to her patrol as if nothing had happened. She looked around for something to contain him. Her uniform hat? Where was her hat? It was on the edge of the open manhole. Her radio had come back to life.

"All units all units, policewoman's hat abandoned by open manhole in Wellesley Road. Full emergency Repeat full emergency. PC 388Zulu – location. Acknowledge. 388Zulu acknowledge.

She heard the sound of sirens and the percussion of chopper blades overhead. If she surfaced, she was in deep shit. If she kept her cool, she'd be in the shit but possibly rich. Frankie sighed in his sleep. She needed a friend.

12 CHAPTER TWELVE

It was useless to call Crispin's mobile. She was sure it would only be a few minutes before a search team was at her door. The police force would go into full operation to find her. Just maybe Crispin would be in his office. She called Scotland Yard and was connected to the media hub office. A male voice answered.

"Is that Crispin?"

"No, the soft twat is in Madrid. Look, I'd like to help but we've a full emergency here. If you're press you need to look lively. This is the story of the century. That woman who did the TV interviews yesterday is missing down a drain. The police have needed something like this for years."

She recognised the voice. This was the guy who'd been at Croydon Police Station ordering the desk sergeant to pull the plugs on Crispin's drag act.

"So, the police *want* this story?"

"Yeah – who are you?"

"Sir, I'm the girl down the drain."

"Yeah right, the book or the film? I've got to get on so what do you want?"

"I'm Selena Fontesse. I'm at my place with Frankie – things got out of control."

Superintendent Bert Brickstone took a deep breath. It was always possible this was a hoax. All the office phones were ringing and the room was filling with bleary-eyed cops dragged out of their beds. Newspapers filled with pictures of Selena Fontesse were on the streets. If ever a situation needed control it was this. This would be his Queen's Police Medal, an extra rank and enhanced pension. He had to get this right.

"OK. Sit tight there, girl. We'll look a proper load of twats if you turn up at home. Don't answer your phone. I'll call off any coppers on the way to your door. Is the ferret alive?"

"Yeah, I've got a chicken leg in the fridge if he's hungry. I think he's been eating rats and mice."

"Don't move, don't answer, don't think. You're a sexy missing police heroine. For now, that's the angle, geddit?"

"I understand. Sir, can you get in touch with Crispin?"

"He'll know soon enough. Give me your address. A plain car will collect you, hopefully before the press get there. Get into civvies and be ready to move. Where's the animal? Does it need a cage?"

"It's sleeping in my bra, sir."

"Look, this is a full cover up operation and I'm taking it on my shoulders. Do not let me down girl. Fuck knows what's in your head. Hear this and hear good. If you get captured before I can get you out of there, play the mental breakdown angle – anything – but go for traumatized victim rather than barking loony. Pressure of fame and attention, difficult childhood, lack of police funds to provide you with support."

"I get it, sir – no rolling eyes and visions."

"Get yourself ready to move."

Bert Brickstone carefully replaced the receiver and made

for his private office. He had to move quickly. He placed a call to the Z-district commander.

"Johnny – it's Bert. You know what's up?"

"Yeah, crazy mad cow's gone off in a Ferrari – we've got the CCTV from the street cams. We've already scooped the driver. He was in the Mayday hospital getting stitches in his dick."

"What's his story?"

"Refuses to talk. Says he caught it in the car door."

"Johnny trust me. We go way back you and me and we both know where the bodies are buried right?"

"I'm listening…,"

"Trash that footage and call off any troops heading for her place. Keep the search going. This woman is a tabloid sensation this morning. There's already queues for veggie tattoos."

"What the fuck Bert?"

"Look, she's alive and she's got Frankie. Whatever the daft bitch has got up to we've got to play this for the tragic missing heroine angle."

The district commander sighed. He had six months to serve before retiring to his villa in Spain.

"Is the commissioner on top of this?"

"Yeah of course," lied Bert, certain it would be a formality.

"OK, I'll do what I have to do. I can't rule out leaks. The job is full of overeducated fuckwits, Trots and snowflakes these days. Selena Fontesse looked like she knew the score in life."

"Females guv… I'll keep you posted."

He knew he was taking too much on his own shoulders. Decisions were like moon-shots. Half an inch out on the launch pad was three hundred miles missing the moon. Once committed – commit. There was one man he could turn to.

He placed the fateful call.

"Nunky?"

"Yeah, who's this?"

"Bert from the lodge."

"Brother... yeah, what?"

"You still got your palace and golf course at Kenley?"

"Yeah, you looking to buy?"

"Nunky, I'm going to give you an address and I want you to get round there now. I want you to pick up a woman and take her to your place. Look after her until I can get there."

"Sounds a bit dodgy, Bert. You over the side with some brass or what?"

"Just do it Nunky and I won't even think of re-opening that file on the bullion job at Heathrow with the chainsaws. You know, the ones some copper traced to your scrapyard. Here's the address and go *now*. Any press or media there just drive on by."

"Bert, as an act of friendship and as a brother I'm on my way."

"You've got a heart of gold Nunks, even if you did nick it."

Bert leaned back in his chair and blew out his cheeks. Once Selena Fontesse was with Nunky Strange the situation was under control. His next call would have to be to the commissioner. Dame Iona Peniston was not his sort of man. He'd not really thought how she would respond. Someone was knocking his office door.

"Yeah, get in and speak quick," he called out.

An androgynous keen press assistant in tight jumper and fashion jeans stepped in.

"Guv' - commissioner wants you to take charge at Croydon. Sir Brandon Pickell is addressing the world's press core over the open manhole as soon as he can land his hot air balloon. He's going to wave his one million cash wad, to show the folk he's not joking."

"Has he ever tried waving even a fiver in public in Croydon? OK. I'm on it."

Like he'd said, half an inch at launch was three hundred miles at the moon. He'd have to brief the commissioner later. He felt the vibration of his mobile in his pocket. It was a text message.

"Got your brass and her pet. Now I know what a polecat's pisser really does smell like. Near miss. Fucking hippy twat just crashed his balloon trying to land in Addiscombe Park. Always here to help a brother. Nunky."

Selena tried to keep her face covered as the Range Rover Vogue picked its way through the fire hoses and rescue equipment spread out across the road. Her companion was a jovial old-ish guy with a mass of gold rings and bracelets. He'd told her his name and shaken hands warmly. He dangled a small cigar from his lips.

"Sorry about the smoke darlin' but that fucking creature hums a bit."

"Shows you how to bath them on Facebook. Where we goin' Nunky?"

"Out to my drum on the Kenley Downs. Right luv'ly it is gal, right ol' bit of class if you know what I'm saying."

Selena smiled. He was obviously a villain but, in the circumstances, so was she.

"How d'you know Bert Brickstone?"

"We're like brothers like – you know, it ain't a woman thing."

"Nunky, do you think I can get away with this?"

"What have you done?"

"I'm a copper. I found Frankie and I nicked him."

"Yeah well, half the world thinks you're a police hero prepared to die to bring joy to a nation in grief."

"What does the other half think?"

"Well, not sure it's my place to say...."

"You don't strike me as shy."

"Well, you'll read the papers anyway. Some say you were a sexpot webcam girl specializing in veggies and vegans. The Guardian is criticizing you for risking life to save a carnivore."

"Jesus Christ mate. How big is that angle?"

"Heroine trumps most things generally my sweetheart. You've been dubbed the *Girl with the Vegan Tattoo* by the Sun."

"So, what has Bert said to you?"

"To look after you until he gets back to me. First thing is to bath little Frankie boy. Then I'm going to chop him up some rabbit fresh off the golf course."

She relaxed back in the seat. Looking down into her lewd male focus area Frankie slept serenely, his little face looking up dreamily into hers.

13 CHAPTER THIRTEEN

Chief Inspector Crispin Bissel had not slept well. He still had not succeeded in removing one eyelash. He had tried to shave with a blunt leg razor and had sliced his chin. He appeared at breakfast in the luxury Villa Real hotel with several patches of toilet paper stuck to his face with blood. Dame Iona Peniston was already in mid Muesli.

"Fucking hell man – this is Madrid. Looks like you've met the barber of Seville," she chortled in amusement at her own posh joke.

"Good morning, ma'am."

"Actually, it is. You spend a career on community initiatives, reaching out, caring and sharing. All a complete load of shit, the more you bend over the more the plebs shaft your ass. Then one morning you wake up to find a trashy trollop has probably got herself drowned down a drain and every police PR dream comes true. The Home Secretary has already nearly doubled our funding."

"Is this all part of the Frankie story?"

"Too right. That blonde from Croydon seems to have gone down a drain and disappeared. All we have is her police hat and an open manhole, but things look bad. There's frogmen searching every inch. No sign of the ferret either by the way."

"Selena Fontesse?"

"That's her. Attractive enough in a brash sort of style."

"There must be hope?"

"Listen, Crispin – yes, but hope for what? I've had a whisper from a secret source in the cabinet office that after the one-hour silence at all football games, The National Cry-In with guest celebrities and the Wembley concert, HM gov' is ditching the ferret. The grief has re-united the nation and we need to sustain that mood. Finding Frankie would kind of re-set the defaults of division between social classes, Brassicas and Romaines, rich and poor. Frankie eats only meat Crispin. He's cute but he's not *one of us*."

He stared down at his own bowl of organic grains and mechanically reached out for the sterilised soya milk.

"Ma'am, Selena was the girl I wanted to marry."

Dame Iona Peniston rolled her eyes and sadly shook her head.

"Bert Brickstone told me you were a soft daft twat. Look, we are Oxford graduate level people, born to command and lead. We are Common Purpose. Believe me, fate has saved you."

"Saved me from love and happiness?"

"Look, of course I'm reaching out and feeling your suffering. We've got to crack on. I've just got to spout the keynote speech on Manchego cheese fraud and then we're heading back for a full COBRA and cabinet meeting. I need to fulfil my destiny to help lead the shiftless mob of noble citizens to sanity. For fuck's sake do something with that eyelash."

He couldn't eat. He thought of Selena alone in the dark, her warm flesh swept away in some stinking current, maybe stuck in a sewage filter and torn by rats. He went to his room, tugged helplessly at his eyelash and gave up. He picked up the room phone and dialled his own number, knowing that his phone was somewhere in her bed-sit. Maybe she'd taken it with her. Oh Selena… please.

Nunky Strange seemed to have found a new passion in his life over and above his taste for armed robbery, rabbit control with a sawn-off shotgun and golf. As Selena held Frankie over the gold-plated sink, filled with warm water and exotic shower gel, Nunky soaped his belly. Frankie crooned in pleasure and general happiness. He'd breakfasted at the table with the humans who'd contented themselves with a fry up.

"That ain't my phone ringing?" said Nunky.

Selena looked back at the table. Someone was calling Crispin. If she ended up nicking the phone, she'd scrap the 'Ode to Joy' ringtone. It wouldn't hurt to accept the call and just listen. She wiped her hands down the front of her jeans and pushed the button.

"Selena… Selena…?"

"Is that *Crispyducks*?"

"Yes, yes, are you alive?"

"Yeah, feels that way. I'm not too pleased with you. Why did you just piss off and not at least tell me you were bailing out of the deal?"

"I was afraid – afraid of all the people against me marrying you. I'm not afraid now. I love you Selena."

"As it goes, *Crispyducks*, I love you. I turned down Carlo Love-God di Rigatoni last night. I could have been wiping sand out of my flaps in the Bay of Naples."

"I'm so glad that didn't happen. I don't understand what's going on and I've got to carry the commissioner's bag to a Manchego cheese conference. I've got to get into my make-up to proclaim inclusivity and equality. Where are you?"

"I'm safe with some mate of Bert Brickstone and I've got Frankie Ferret. No one wants me to be alive. It's a full cover up job to spin the police hero angle."

"I want you alive and no one else matters. I love you so much Selena. I shouldn't tell you this but there's whispers that the bosses are junking Frankie."

"He's adorable. There's no way they're going to take him down while I'm alive."

"I'm back this afternoon for a top-level meeting. I'll talk to Bert Brickstone and somehow, I'll get to you. Don't answer my phone again but keep an eye on my phone for texts. I love you."

"If you let me down again, I'll set Frankie on your dick *Crispyducks*. He likes a bit of red meat. I love you too."

As he clicked off, she ran through his messages. She read the last one.

Darling, that awful woman you talked about is missing, looks like dead. Once it's confirmed you need to proclaim your loss and sorrow. Go big on the victim position and I've got media contacts to really spin your suffering. This could make you so big. Thinking of you, Mummy xxxx

Was everything just spin and PR? She had a feeling that *Mummy* was not going to be best pleased unless Crispin failed her again. For some reason this time she trusted him and, and in any event, quite simply, she loved him.

Chief Inspector Bissel applied the other eyelash and his lip gloss. He needed to improve his cosmetic skills if he was going to go much further as an inclusion icon. All the same he had a spring in his step as he carried the commissioner's briefcase into the grand convention centre. As he smiled in the background at all times making notes and nodding agreement behind his boss, one thing played on his mind. It was obvious that Dame Iona Peniston was outside the loop. As she spoke sadly about the loss of one of the finest officers in the police service, she believed what she was saying. She wasn't part of the cover up. He would have to play his hand with skill, but he had the powerful hand of knowledge.

The conference was quickly over. There was a group photo and a joint communique about the importance of brand integrity, particularly regarding Manchego cheese. A guy from the Emmental Tendency group of Euro MPs, presented an inscribed crystal plaque in the shape of a block of cheese complete with holes which Crispin had to carry to the plane with his free hand. Once aboard the commissioner looked at her award.

"Bloody trash – they know I'm a vegan so it's just a piss-take by some amateur spin agency to try and trap me. Just get rid of it," she ordered.

Crispin nodded and settled into writing up the notes of the conference. His leader kept an extensive diary ready for the compilation of her memoirs, already commissioned by Blabber and Blabber of Bloomsbury. This was his sole duty other than bag-carrying and inclusivity eye-candy. When he'd finished, he checked out the posh newspapers provided on the plane. The Times ignored ferrets and proclaimed 'Crimea Breakthrough. Eurovision Babushkas Pull Out'. As the convoy swept them back to Scotland Yard, he noticed wreaths and bouquets on every drain and gulley. Pictures of Frankie with a range of celebrities were attached to lampposts. Everyone was wearing "Je Suis Frankie" T-shirts while street vendors sold key rings and black arm bands. Tomorrow was the weekend with events planned in every corner of the land. The Northern Ireland Assembly had reached agreement to come together during the emergency. The bells of churches would start tolling at dawn with the theme tune from Frankie's TV show. Every footballer in all leagues had pledged to point skyward and to his Frankie shirt logo to dedicate every goal to his being. He decided to take a small initiative.

"Ma'am, may I ask about the planned future of the ferret? You mentioned perhaps he'd served his purpose. I'm catching some population expectation management vibes on the street – the black arm bands, the football stars pointing to heaven, the tolling bells. Surely there is still hope?"

"Looks that way to me too. You mustn't overplay this stuff to the drongs because *even they* can notice too much hype. That hetero casting-couch creep Vandervel O' Brien is leading a lot of the public wailing. His films are popular, but he just has to hammer it in. It's torture to people at our level just because it's so obvious. He's got them chanting "Frankie Ferret long and sable, long and sable.""

"We studied his Red Flag of the Grimethorpe Zombies at Oxford as an icon of pre-populism."

"Huh – populism, that shit. It's the dictatorship of the proletariat on fucking Love Island. If the policewoman – your friend, isn't found, then Frankie's always going to be the cause of her death and he loses all victim kudos himself. If she is found, then it's all anti-climax and back to strife as normal."

"Ma'am, in an ideal world, in a Common Purpose mindset – you know for people like us, what would be your dream play out on this?"

"Simple. Dead ferret, hero cop. I can tell by your question that you're an Oxford boy. Leadership and command – never forget it Crispin. I'm thinking we'll know a lot more after the meeting with the PM. I want you at my side. I'm seeing a good mind in that painted head of yours. Now as soon as we get to my office step in and sort my hair out. I've got my own electric clippers to shave the top but it's a sod reaching the back. I want to look at my best for what lies ahead."

In an odd way Crispin was beginning to like her. They were becoming almost intimate. After all, he'd been bred to be among people like this. If only he'd never met Selena Fontesse. He wondered what would happen if he told her everything he knew. He was only twenty-four and maybe his innocence urged him to continue.

"Ma'am, what if Selena, my fiancée after all, what if she were to be found alive with Frankie at this moment?"

"It would be a pain in the ass. Look at these people broken by grief. They're fucking loving it. They're all victims. They're all famous. Victimhood is the highest possible status. These fucking idiots are trying to out sob each other. My sorrow is greater than yours. My wailing is louder than yours, my tears are hotter than yours, blah blah blah. It's emotion without consequence, it's social harmony without equalisation of wealth."

"I see your drift Ma'am. If they did materialize in some way would we cover it up?"

She nodded, smiled and fixed him with an unnerving certainty in her eyes.

"That's a question for politics Crispin. My hope would be yes, but I'd keep my own nose clean. The PM is a scoundrel. He's the sort of man we would need in that level of crisis. I'm catching something in the wind from you. That Bert Brickstone has been trying to call me. He's sent messages saying there's something I need to know about the situation but I'm kind of guessing it for myself. The Z-district commander tells me the CCTV footage is missing. It'd better stay that way I think. Come on, let's sort out my hair. How do you think I'd look with a flat-top?"

14 CHAPTER FOURTEEN

Superintendent Bert Brickstone waited impatiently out of frame while Sir Brandon Pickell posed with his wad of cash over the manhole. A clamouring crowd had gathered, and extra police had been called in from outside London. Several young folk had broken through cordons to offer him their CVs, one young lady having typed details of her Duke of Edinburgh awards and scouting achievements on her panties. To be fair, the great man had smiled and gently blessed all the candidates. At last he was ushered away to his electrically powered pale green eco stretch-limo.

Bert retreated to his office and pulled out his bottle of Chivas Regal, taking a swig straight from the neck. The whole machine was flat out and still the decision rested on his shoulders alone. He had superiors but no one from his own stable of humanity. Most higher bosses were clean young management college kids who spent most of their time scheming ways to rid the Force of dinosaurs like him. He flicked through his pocket diary and address book. There was one man he knew but hardly dared to approach. His heart pounded as the number connected and began to ring.

A strong male voice answered.

"Yes. Who is this?"

"I believe a secret between two men is a secret of God, sir."

"I agree, identify yourself as what you are," answered Basil Montacute-Jones.

"Character is what a man is in the dark, sir." said Bert.

"Well get the fuck into the light and speak of our acquaintance."

"I once served god and her majesty as a humble officer on the fraud squad, sir. I once had a mission to attend the share dealing desk of the Sackman-Platinum bank on the square mile of London. I recall a fine citizen by your name, sir."

"Fuck my boots. Bert Brickstone. I thought you'd be golfing with all the other old soaks by now. Glad to know you're on the level brother."

"Sir, I need to discuss a matter with you. I'm working at the media hub of Scotland Yard."

"And you want me to shag Iona Peniston to put a smile on her face," laughed the PM.

"Optional, sir. I'm dealing with that ferret and I'd like to share certain confidences."

"Bertie boy – come round to Number Ten. Got a single malt here longing for some company worth sharing. I've got to talk to Pinupskin about the Crimea conference, and I'll have the drinks set up by the time you can trot round. There's a full hour before the COBRA meeting. Good man."

Bert muttered a silent prayer of thanks. And he was going to get a drink.

Thirty minutes later the Prime Minister leaned back in his winged chair, making a steeple of his fingers.

"Thank Christ for you old foxes Bertie. Maybe I should

say Sir Bertie, QPM, maybe OBE – you choose. I've levelled with you and I'm trusting you. All the honours are dependent on you pulling this off. You're sure the old bat doesn't know?"

"My guess, doesn't want to know, sir."

"Good enough. She's one of the wily elite. Now, you can guarantee getting the ferret and that woman out of sight, for ever? Everything is committed to the Reign of the Bear just as soon as that concert closes. I want the plebs back at their workplaces with all this behind them on Monday morning. The GDP is down half a percent and the markets are twitching."

"Yes. The only possible hitch is the woman's supposed fiancé. He's that tranny cop on the cover of PC magazine this morning. He's straight but he's the personal aide to Iona Peniston."

"Look, can we pay him off?"

Bert tried to imagine the mindset of Crispin Bissel. It was like a sunflower trying to explain solar radiation to Vincent Van Gogh.

"Sir, the woman wanted the ferret to get Brandon Pickell's million quid. If we could get that money –,"

"Leave all that to me Bertie boy. I'm going to talk to the guy directing the show on Sunday. Things could fall very well into place for us. I've got an idea and I do believe I'm something of a genius."

As soon as Sir Bert Brickstone OBE QPM was clear of Number Ten, the PM placed a call.

"Pickell old boy, thanks so much for all you're doing. I've got a proposition for you."

"Yah, that sounds sooper cool."

"Five percent on Viktor the bear cub. I need you to pay out that reward up front if you agree – full tax deduction if you understand me and total world spotlight. Dinner tonight at my club to close?"

"Hey Baz, yah sure, that's Gucci."

The PM grimaced as he rang off. Sir Pickell had appeared five times on the honours shortlist for Lord and five times he'd crossed him off out of personal dislike. By chance it meant that if the deal snagged tonight, he'd have that extra sweetie in his pocket.

Back at Scotland Yard, Bert wasn't surprised to find a note on his desk asking him to go immediately to the commissioner's office. As he entered, he was slightly nonplussed at the sight of a uniformed Chief Inspector in full drag make-up wielding a pair of budget Aldi home clippers as he cut Dame Iona Peniston's dark greying hair.

"We've gone for a flat top and really severe sides Bert. What do you think?" she asked.

"You look like a bleeding aircraft carrier for wasps," he said.

"But does it look strong and uncompromising?"

"Yeah, I'd go for that."

"Great job Crispin. Get the floor brush out of the corner and get the loose bits off my head. I've never been one for all that fem fairy shit," she said.

"Me too," Bert responded.

The commissioner shrieked with laughter.

"Better hashtag that – ha ha – geddit?" she added, noting his blank look. "Now, this awful tragedy with that officer sucked out to sea on the tide from the sewage outfall. I think we should keep hope alive but scale back the commitment of manpower. Knife crime has stopped since Frankie went missing but it won't last."

"Ma'am we don't know what happened to her."

"Yes, they tell me she could have gone through the

macerators and been settled out in the sludge beds. Poor cow is probably spread as manure on a skunk weed farm in Essex by now."

"What level of manpower would you want to continue?"

"Well, you stay with it yourself to handle media. Use the specials – they love to feel useful and involved and we can pay their wages."

"We don't pay them Ma'am."

"You don't say? There's a vacancy with an extra rank coming up on the mayor's finance committee Bert. Sounds like you've got the clarity of mind to step in there."

Bert stroked his chin. His look of fox regarding chicken matched her interpretation of heron watching goldfish. He knew that she knew. She knew that he knew she knew. Crispin busied himself with packing up the haircutter.

"So, Ma'am, I'm gathering that I can deal with this matter and keep it in the public eye for a while yet but, we are preparing the public to accept the demise of all parties as a pragmatic act of kindness."

"Absolutely Bert. I know I can trust you to leave no loose ends. We have to move on, grow our consciousness, cry our tears and unite in grief over this weekend ahead. Then it's crack the whip and get the world running again. It would be unfortunate if we deviated from this schedule at this late stage. PC Selena Fontesse will be immortal and a beacon to all women."

"And Frankie?" asked Crispin.

"Frankie is a fucking stupid ferret. His fame is because some religious kid with a hot PR team heard him say *Amen*. There are no magic animals Crispin."

"Not even unicorns?"

"Police don't do politics. Now let's get to the COBRA meeting. Bert, tell the folks out there the tale. Do what you have to do."

15 CHAPTER FIFTEEN

Nunky Strange watched a police car swing into the car park outside his country mansion. He'd left Selena asleep in bed with Frankie nuzzled between her womanly bosom. He had to admit she was a fair bit of brass but a bit modern feisty for his liking. He strolled out to meet his old mucker Superintendent Brickstone of the Sweeney.

"Good on ya, bro," he said exchanging a warm handshake. Dusk was falling and from what he'd read, the ferret would soon be hungry and active. He lifted a dead rabbit off the fence where he'd hung it to drain the blood. Nunky Strange had known hunger and what meat he'd had as a kid had been rabbit off Hackney Marshes or rump steak nicked by his mum in Sainsbury's.

"You come to see your lady friend?"

"Yeah and you Nunky. You still got a plane?"

"I might have –,"

"I won't beat about the bush. I may ask you to fly out the brass, the tranny boyfriend and the ferret."

"Where to?"

"I'm working on that. Look mate, thanks for what you did this morning. If I can repay you in any way?"

"Twenty grand should do it. I charge a bit more for flying under radar with no lights at night."

"How much more."

"Ten million cos I ain't that brave or daft. A nice little pleasure flight to Normandy or Brittany is well possible. I regularly re-locate assets in that spirit of European free movement."

"I don't want to know."

"But if I did encounter an issue, perhaps I could call you Bert?"

"Yeah, let's make a deal on that. One free pass and that's all."

The two men shook hands again.

"How much notice for a flight, Nunky?"

"I'll hold my social calendar open all day tomorrow. Remember it's winter and daylight is crucial."

"I need to talk to her. How's she been?"

"Mate, she's lovely but she stinks a bit of ferret. She's showered four times. Bloody animal won't come out from between her tits."

Selena was stirring. Frankie was nibbling at her chin and squeaking.

"Tell Mummy what you want," she said softly.

Frankie made no sensible response except trying to pull the duvet onto the floor. He scratched at the door with a certain urgency.

"Frankie want *pee-pee?*"

"Amen. Amen," said Frankie.

She gathered him up and went to the bathroom. She sat Frankie in the bidet and plonked herself on the toilet. Together they obtained release.

"Frankie want munchies?" she asked.

"Amen," said the ferret.

She dressed, let Frankie get comfortable in her lewd male focus area and wandered out to find her host.

"This 'orrible bald geezer is Bert Brickstone. Not sure if you've met?" he said.

She recognised him from the police station press conference.

"Nice to meet you, sir."

"So that animal poking his little chops out of your bra is Frankie?"

"He's the TV kid's show representation of Frankie. He's like Thomas the Tank Engine with musk glands and a bladder. The real Frankie is in a kid's book. He saved some poor miner. But of course, it's just a name and words but it's kind of real at the same time."

"Post-modernism, the simulacrum, the blurring of image and reality," said Nunky.

"Fuck off Nunks, where did you get that lot?" said Bert

"Studied philosophy in Parkhurst on a seven stretch. Got three years remission for my thesis on the decline of liberal democracy."

"Jesus! If I'd known that I'd have put my idle son in Parkhurst to get his media studies degree."

"Nah, they stopped that cos they want degrees where you can get a job after," Nunky explained.

Bert smiled at Selena. She really was quite lovely.

"Darlin' I'll come to the point. You're set up to be an immortal beacon to all women –,"

"What about men – can I be a unisex or bi-sexual beacon? To be honest I'd rather be a role model and inspiration to all of humanity."

"All of them I promise. We'll give it whatever spin you want on the day."

"So yeah, what happens to me?"

"We fly you out of England with Frankie if you want to take him. You disappear."

"Like left in a street somewhere disgusting like Brussels with no money and a ferret to feed and bring up? I don't think so mate."

"Somewhere nice. You'll get the reward money and I'll keep you on the payroll as a cop. We trash your old identity and life resets."

"Deal, on one condition."

"I'm listening?"

"Two conditions. Crispin comes too and he marries me."

"I can't make him marry you."

"That's my conditions. If not, I'll face up to what I've done, walk into a cop shop, confess and surrender."

"Why you stupid cow?" interjected Nunky.

"Cos I love him, *geddit?*"

Bert reached out and took her hand.

"I'll work on it. Relax and give me overnight. I'll call you in the morning before eight o'clock. You need anything?"

"Frankie's hungry. Can you fry him a bit of bunny Nunks?" she said.

"Let's settle in people," began the Prime Minister as he opened the COBRA meeting in the underground war rooms. "We've come through a very challenging time and I'm proud, yes proud of you all."

The newly appointed Lord Legume stood up.

"Here here, Basil, we're proud of you too. If I can quote Saint Francis the Ass, 'Where there were doubts you brought certainty. Where there were ferrets you brought us bears'."

"Yes, yes thank you. Now cut the grovelling and pin your ears back. The ferret is finished. Any dissent after Sunday night is heresy. It was always total carnivore and some of those involved in the cover up may face consequences. As any right-minded free-thinking British soldier will tell you, you can't rely on those above to save you if you just follow orders. If we have to smear Frankie because of reactionary heretics we won't hesitate. A government leak to the BBC Pornarama show could reveal operatives who rolled out chicken breasts and sprayed them green to look like lettuce. My deal with Russia on Viktor the Bear has solved the Ukraine conflict. I fly to Paris to hammer out a pact with Pinupskin on Monday. I want you all to relax over the weekend and enjoy the event. Every cabinet member is expected to attend the silences, the flower laying by the Queen in Whitehall and the cry-ins. If you can't get to Wembley for the concert, be in front of your screens. This will be special. Don Trumpeone is flying in with some of his boys. Special songs have been written. Gretchen Thunderbird has flown in by glider towed by a British Airbus 320. Sir Brandon Pickell is showing us what an inspiration he is to us all. Be there or spend the rest of your days rending your vestments and gnashing your hair. In the front of our hearts and minds remains the beautiful heroic missing officer even though the dark shades of night kind of colour in her face with a weird heavy pencil effect. I believe a mangled police style shoe has been recovered at the Beddington sewage treatment works. Let your tears water the furrows of public virtue colleagues. The next hours will write our legacy in history."

The meeting closed. Crispin picked up the commissioner's bag and walked with her to her car.

"Ma'am, may I finish my duty for the day?"

"No stamina I see, but yes. Join me at 0630. I'm doing a Saturday morning TV show in what was the Frankie slot. Gotta keep the kids onside Crispin."

He watched her walk away and sat down on a low wall

waiting to catch Bert Brickstone. It wasn't a long wait.

"Thank Christ you're there Bissel. You have the future of this nation in your hands my son and I kid you not. Come and get in my car. I've been waiting for you. We're going for a spin out in the country."

"Why?"

"Cos you're going to get married to the *Girl with the Vegan Tattoo* like you've always wanted to, leave England with a million quid and save the nation."

Crispin slumped into the back seat of the government Jaguar XF. All his education screamed that this was wrong and stupid. Every bone and fibre of his body was ready to accept.

"Yes. OK then, where do I sign?"

"What no protests about human rights, workplace bullying and abuse of power?"

"Yeah but fuck it. I'll do it."

"OK, we're stopping off in Streatham to pick up some sort of vicar. He's a bit of a soak, but a brother nonetheless. He's sorted out all the papers and he looks the business with dog collar and some holy water."

"What's the water for?"

"In case the fucking ferret wants a drink you twat. How should I know? I ain't into god-bothering. Why are you accepting this so easy?"

"Cos I trust you, Bert. I know you'll never rat on me or blow me out. The day you grabbed my ass in the bog at Wetherspoon's I went back and seized the CCTV cassette and you have no idea where it is or how many copies I've got. I trust you with my life Bert."

"OK, son, let's not dwell there but thanks for that information. Let's get that vicar and get the job done."

"I need to phone my mother."

Bert handed him his phone.

"Mummy, I need some help. I need a place to go, somewhere foreign, discrete and ferret friendly. I would use TripAdvisor but there's no match on ferret. You have contacts all over Europe."

"What madness is this darling?"

"It's the madness of love. I'm marrying Selena."

"She's dead."

"She won't accept mortality."

"Only because her limited uneducated vocabulary doesn't know the word."

"So, can you help me? If I slip away into obscurity you won't be shamed. I'm going to do it anyway and perhaps I'll make a splash."

He heard his mother sighing and stifling sobs. She'd left him with a nanny when he was ten months old to work as an advisor at the Strasbourg parliament, so he'd hardened his heart to her endless sorrow at his lack of ambition.

"Look, a scandal like this could wreck my MEP career. I'm leader of the Progressive Demagogue Group and vice chair of the Endangered Red Herring Fishery Commission. There is one person, but you must never, never, let this be known. It's your Aunt Emma."

"I haven't got an Aunt Emma."

"Yes, you have. She's my younger sister. We no longer talk about her."

"I'm intrigued…."

"Darling we didn't want you to know. She's Emma Calin the novelist. She invented Frankie Ferret years and years ago when she was a writer for children. She's regarded as a very attractive woman and your dear father very much liked her mental company. He was doing some intellectual thought shows for BBC radio and sometimes stayed with her at her London boudoir, merely to save all the stress of coming home late and waking me when his mind was aching with thought at such a high level. He talked them in to picking up Frankie for a TV show. That's how the wretched thing went global. That's how she has a vineyard and chateau in France."

"Well that's not shameful."

"No, but she got bored and started writing dreadful books all about unspeakable lust. She's a best seller but it's unreadable to people like us. It's non inclusive. It's totally hetero – 'hunks and humping' she calls it. Now she's a dreadful brash woman worshiped by male and female readers of basically classy porn."

"So, she's Frankie's mum. That's just so cool."

"Darling the only hairy animal things she's actually touched are too awful to talk about."

"Can you call her?"

"Yes, yes, I'll get back to you. She's the only person I know who's dishonourable enough to enjoy such shame."

"Love you Mummy," he said as she hung up.

16 CHAPTER SIXTEEN

The ceremony was small but dignified. Nunky lent Selena a designer wedding dress, one of several he'd kept stashed in his loft after his gang had accidentally drilled through a mural wall signed 'Banksy' and ended up in a bridal shop instead of a money vault. Crispin looked smart enough in his Chief Inspector's uniform. Bert and Nunky stood as witnesses for the ceremony in the mansion's snooker room, the table utilised as an altar bearing a cross brought by the vicar from his own tabernacle. Frankie spent most of the service asleep, peering dreamily out of Selena's bra, his cute tiny paws holding him up to get a view of the priest's features. He remained dormant but repeated "Amen" when it was time to join in. The wedding feast was a delivered Chinese blow out, revealing Frankie's addiction to king prawns. Finally, it was time to consummate the union.

"I kind of feel he's watching me," said Crispin, his broad shoulders above her, dominating, controlling and teasing her pulsing lust. Frankie gazed up from Selena's lewd male focus area, eyes closed. Crispin drove on to the joy he craved.

"That was fantastic, I love you," he said.

"Amen," murmured Frankie in his sleep.

Basil Montacute-Jones shook hands with Sir Brandon Pickell as they split from their dinner rendezvous at his club. The only sticking point had been the unconditional surrender of the million pounds reward. Basil patted the wad in his pocket as he slipped into his Bentley behind the chauffeur. His guest had already left on his electric bicycle, carrying a doggy bag of lentils to re-heat in his solar cell oven for breakfast. Everything was set to go. After this pleb-soaked madness he could travel to Paris on Monday to secure the accord with Russia which he knew from inside sources would bag him the Nobel Prize. Then he could sit back, write his memoirs, settle all the scores with rivals and live off the financial frenzy around both Frankie Ferret and Viktor the Bear. He slept well, dreaming just maybe of a talking panda called Basil.

Crispin Bissel took an early call from his mother that Sunday morning. He had ignored his phone and ratted on his deadline with the commissioner at 6.30am. The die was cast.

"Crispin your father and I love you. Your ghastly Aunt Emma will be delighted to see you. She has arranged for a landing at a small airfield near Marrennes in south west France. Her chateau of shame is close by. She will meet you there with upright bicycles, hooped jumpers and berets. She will then cycle you undercover to her estate. She will house you in a cottage and employ you as proof-readers of her ghastly filth. Yes or no?"

"Yes of course. Text me her number. I'll call her as we take off. I love you too Mummy and Pater."

He leaned to kiss his bride to be met by Frankie reaching out to stroke his cheek. The smell was powerful, yet he was beginning to like it.

THE KINGDOM PAUSED AND TOOK A MOMENT TO LOOK BACK AT WHAT HAD HAPPENED. A PEOPLE FUSED IN SORROW HELD HANDS AND VIRTUE-SIGNALLED TO THE GALAXY.

GOD GLANCED AND GOT ON WITH GROWING THE MODEL OF UNIVERSAL EXPANSION IN THE CONTEXT OF A CONSUMER DRIVEN SLOWDOWN. IT WAS FUCKING TOUGH AS THE TOP ECONOMIST WHEN DESIRE FAILED TO INCITE GREED.

The day had been a triumph. All the public ceremonies had gone well. The BBC had dedicated all channels to rolling repeats of the one-hour silence. ITV had organised a regional contest for the best shrines. The archbishop of Britain had gone live from Westminster Abbey with a special Christmas sermon entitled 'Gold, Frankie Sense and Fur'. Thousands had jammed into Saint Peter's Square in Rome to hear the pope chant the 'Mustelidus Angelicus'. Slowly the clock had dragged round to the moment of the climax of the day – the Wembley concert. World TV and beyond went live. The rock bands wailed out their anthems – the Sister Sledge song 'Frankie Do You Remember Me?' played and played. The giant screens fizzed with loops of Frankie TV shows. Stewards carried collapsed and overwhelmed citizens from the emotion-drenched crowd. Opportunistic vendors sold pots of saline and glycerine tears labelled as 'Viagra for Exhausted Tear Ducts'. The great market of humanity triumphed over grief and held out its hand for payment. As the Red Barrow pilots finished their eco green run-past up the field, there appeared a pink prince of genius on the stage at a piano shaped like a ferret, the teeth in his open mouth forming the keyboard. A seemingly vulnerable child with shaven head and staring eyes was led by robed officials from the Primate Rebellion school of bishops. Millions wanted to reach out to comfort the child as she openly wept and trembled. The priests bowed at her feet as the music started to play. Gretchen Thunderbird raised her eyes to the sky. Her head mic' picked up her cries of terror. At first the music was a rewrite of an old tune, 'Frankie is leaving tonight on a plane...'. The stadium lights extinguished. In the darkness countless thousands waved their mobile phones and lighters.

"And I can see Frankie waving goodbye...," sang the band.

Gretchen Thunderbird reached out desperately as if to hold him, maybe even pull him back. The giant screens flashed into life. Sir Brandon Pickell was in his balloon, ascending into heaven. He was in robes and holding a small coffin in his outstretched arms towards the cameras. The coffin containing the heart of a people's love, of the need to share and externalise emotion in the absence of any genuine mass experience other than the choreographed illusions of entertainment. A people immunized against truth and mortality, only able to respond to treatment from above by Doctor Good.

The music beat changed. The crowd hushed. A great one sang.

"Goodbye Frankie boy... like a ferret in the wind...,"

The hot air balloon ascended and ascended. Brandon Pickell raised the tiny casket towards the hands of god as they disappeared into cloud. Gretchen Thunderbird screamed out to halt the agony of her loss. The crowd started to chant.

"Frankie Ferret long and sable. Frankie Ferret long and sable...,"

On and on it went and until the words made no sense and began to become a wild mantra of incomprehension. The producers caught the danger of the chanting mob and cued in the EU anthem. Gretchen Thunderbird fell to uncontrollable hysterical tears. The Primate Rebellion priests moved in to hold her as she convulsed. She raised her hands and the adults threw themselves aside. As the spotlights homed in on her she looked to the skies, her hands wide, her face lit by joy.

"I see a ring of fire. I see the stars of the Little Bear. I see a flaming word like *Tennessee*. I see Frankie sparkling on a sequined cloak."

Abruptly she collapsed as the bishops and scribes rushed in to interpret and record her vision. The Sun reporter filed his copy:

'Frankie is with Elvis. Official.'

Other interpretations of this story are available and will be forever. And ever. Amen.

FIN

FREE DOWNLOAD

Bag a FREE ebook when you
join Oscar's Reader Club

Hungry For More?

**Get this title
FREE
When you join
Oscar for exclusive
fun features,
competitions and
bargain comedy books
at the
'SUCK IT UP CLUB'**

*"A poignant story celebrating
life's heroes"*

Follow the QR code link or visit:
https://smarturl.it/CoverSuckItUp

A MESSAGE FROM OSCAR

Thank you for reading this story. I hope you enjoyed it. If would be wonderful if you could post a review for me. Either drop me an email, to oscar@gallo-romano.co.uk, or post on your favourite review site.

I cannot compete with the big guys who employ complex machines and budgets to promote their titles, but your feedback helps other readers find my work and means so much to me. Thank you.

Hoping to share more with you in the very near future.
Regards,
Oscar

P.S. To meet Frankie Ferret in his original children's story click this link: or use the QR code.

https://smarturl.it/FindFrankie

FREE BOOKS

If you enjoy my writing, why not keep up to date with my new releases, giveaways and competitions by joining my VIP Reader Group **'The Suck It Up Club'**?

I'll send you a copy of my short story 'Champions' as a welcome gift. Click the image or the link below, or use the QR code to join my club now:

https://smarturl.it/CoverSuckItUp

As a valued reader, you'll get exclusive freebies, special offers, goodies and giveaways, un-published extras and the chance to get pre-release editions of my new books before they go on general release. There might even be a chance for you to get your name (or one of your friends!) into my next book as a supporting character

You just can't get this stuff anywhere else.

I like to reach out several times each month with news and bargains, but don't worry, I won't bombard you and will never share your details. You may of course unsubscribe at any time.

MORE BOOKS BY OSCAR SPARROW

CHAMPIONS

http://www.smarturl.it/WebChampions

A short story about a time when the colour of the jeans you wore defined your tribe.

POETRY
I THREW A STONE

https://smarturl.it/OscarStone

FREEZE FRAME

https://smarturl.it/OscarFreeze

Both titles are available in ebook, print and audiobook formats. Poetry reorded by the poets themselves with original music composition leitmotifs.

ABOUT OSCAR SPARROW

Oscar Sparrow was born in Winchester UK in 1949, apparently thanks to the American Marshal Aid program to re-build Europe after the war. As the colour red leached its way out of the map of the British Empire, Oscar attended a die-hard Church school designed to create noble savages to serve what was left of the savage Nobles. The Eleven Plus exam revealed that he could not even count to eleven and he became a mechanic, labourer, truck driver, boxer and poet. He read Wordsworth and Ford Cortina manuals in a lorry cab near both Oxford and Cambridge universities. He married a kind forgiving woman who eventually forgave herself for that one big mistake. He has several wonderful children and hopes that one day they will all meet.

At the age of 25 he heard the music of Edith Piaf and learned to sing all her songs. A few years later he realised she was French and that he was an ugly swan not a beautiful duckling. The shock propelled him to London where he joined the Metropolitan Police. Car chases and riots followed but he did not take it personally. He spent his spare time touring the Art galleries, singing Piaf and learning Italian. Eventually, The Authorities fell for the con and gave him a desk job in the Art department of Interpol London at Scotland Yard.

One day a few years later, the lure of the wild swept him away to the roads of Europe as road gipsy trucker. His love of fried battered fish eventually drew him back to England where he drove sewage tankers and set up a taxi business.

FIND OSCAR SPARROW ON THE INTERNET

Blog: https://oscarsparrow.wordpress.com/

Twitter: https://twitter.com/Oscar_Sparrow

Facebook Fan Page:
https://www.facebook.com/TheTurdMan/

YouTube: http://www.youtube.com/OscarSparrowWriter

Instagram: https://www.instagram.com/virtualbookcafe/

BookBub: https://www.bookbub.com/profile/OscarSparrow

Amazon Author Link: http://www.smarturl.it/AmazonSparrow

PUBLISHER

This book was published by Gallo-Romano Media. For details of other books and authors or if you would like to submit your book for publishing:

Email: contact@gallo-romano.co.uk
Web: http://www.gallo-romano.co.uk